The Chosen
Prophecy's End

The Chosen
Prophecy's End

by
C.A. Milson

First Published 2019 ASJ Publishing

www.asjpublishing.com

" Then the fifth [angel] emptied his bowl on the throne
of the beast, and his kingdom was [plunged] in darkness;
and people gnawed their tongues for the torment [of their
excruciating distress and severe pain]."

—Revelation of John 16:10

"In the days of the last, the king of perdition shall arise
from the belly of slumber. And his armies reap the land like
a sower harvests the fields. Lo, a storm from the heavens
come and his lands and tribes shall be thrown into the
abyss of eternal darkness."

—Azullrokr the Prophet 14:7.
Book of Mezunabite. 5,308BC

Prologue

ALEX AWOKE TO find himself in a vast valley. He slowly rose to his feet. In every direction he looked, he saw nothing but a vast barren wasteland and pockets of steam rising from the warm ground. He glanced up at the sky, and only saw that thick impenetrable darkness.

He sighed heavily; he knew exactly where he was.

"Fuck," he whispered. And then he screamed it as loud as he could. "*Fuck*!" He was in the depths of Tanzac's world, and somewhere in this place, his alter-ego was on the loose. "Fuck this!" he screamed again. The echo trailed off, softening into the distance.

He closed his eyes and tried to use his power to teleport out of this fucking place, but he could not. He was trapped. Stranded. Helpless. Abandoned in a wasteland to face a dark realm of insanity where nothing was ever as it seemed.

Everywhere he looked offered any hope. Yet, somewhere in this world, he knew that Usher and Drake were also here, experiencing their own personal hell. He hoped that somehow, if at all possible, he would be able to find them and release them.

Right now, the only thing he was destined to do was fight with what little power he had, liberate the captives, and put an end to Tanzac. If, indeed, he could. He had already failed to defeat the Son of the Dusk so many times. Judging from his current situation, he failed to see how another bout in the ring would have any different outcome. This was Tanzac's world, and here Tanzac *was* god.

~

ALEX LOOKED AROUND again, noticing the dark mountains that lay in each direction. Every way he looked, there seemed to be no way out, and no one to hear him. He shrugged and decided to walk off toward what he thought would be north. Little did he know that even now, as he trudged through this wasteland, he was fulfilling his own destiny, and his own prophecy was soon to end.

Alex was not as alone as he thought. Far ahead, in a remote cavern inside the distant mountains, his alter-ego sat and waited for his arrival. His alter-ego was powerful, and he had the power to kill the last of the bloodline of a forgotten race once and for all. And there was nothing that the Elders could do to interfere. Here, the Elders had no place.

As Alex walked towards the distant mountains, he secretly hoped this was nothing more than a dream. But he knew that this wasn't, and he knew he wouldn't easily find a way back into the real world. Everything in his world, in his time, was gone. This realm was timeless, eternal, and the torment of the millions of souls suffering went on without rest.

1

DRAKE ARRIVED IN this god forsaken hell 15 years ago, but to him, those 15 years seemed to be an eternity. An eternity of darkness, suffering, agony and endless torment.

There were times he hoped and groaned to be back in the real world, drinking ice cold beers with his friends and planning his next TV adventure. But all such hope was futile. His lot was to be tormented endlessly by the demons that haunted him in this darkness. He was bound, in a shallow pit, with lava dripping on his eternal soul, with each drip sending agonizing pain through his whole being, and the screams of his agony filled the silence around him, echoing off into the distance. But here, no one heard his screams for help. No one could hear his agony. He was alone in the darkness... to suffer, alone.

Drake lay there, bound, his eyes darting to and fro with fear and pain evident in his glare, he saw no one. His fate seemed to be sealed.

USHER SAT QUIETLY in the dark room and looked around when his eyes adjusted to the darkness around him, he could see that he was in a waiting room of sorts. Much like the one he was in before when he went on a screaming match. The reception desk was nearby ahead of him, and somewhere to his right, the entrance to the hospital.

He knew where he was. It may have appeared that he was still in that hospital. But he knew better than that.

He held his head in the palms of his hands and sighed.

"For the love of..." He muttered softly. "Drake. Forgive me brother."

He felt almost hungover, but he knew that he was neither hungover nor was he really in that hospital. He knew that he was in Tanzac's world, reliving his own personal hell and facing his own demons. As fearful as he should have been, Usher was wiser than his enemy expected, and Usher used that fear to gather his own strength to see the reality of what was going on.

"Drop down on the floor now!" He suddenly heard someone demand nearby. He looked up and glanced around, and saw no one. Slowly he stood up and peered off into the direction he heard the voice. No one. He looked back the other way.

Nothing.

"Lutancix". He muttered, almost expecting to see that foolish little demon appear from out of the darkness. But he did not.

Suddenly, there were the sounds of gunfire from behind him. Usher quickly turned around and again, no one.

"Fuck this. I'm off." He muttered, as he started toward the entrance. He needed to make sense of this world... this place, if he was to keep his sanity.

～ゝ

USHER WENT OVER to the door and tried to push it open. Locked. He huffed to himself and tried to look beyond that hazed gray glass. There was nothing he could see beyond that thick glass door. Even the windows on either side of the door were covered with that thick gray-like mist. It was as though he had no choice but to remain in this place.

Again, he tried to force the door open to no avail. It was pointless. But being hard-headed as he was, rather than just give up straight away, he decided to grab a nearby chair and try throwing it through the glass, only to have the same result as his previous attempt.

Nothing.

"Fuck this shit." He said loud enough to be heard by the sound of his own echo.

He glanced around the foyer and started to wonder if there was any point in doing anything.

"I sure could use a drink right now."

He went and sat back down and looked around once again. He sighed, knowing that he was … alone.

Alex was tired, afraid. He had no idea where he was going, but with each step there seemed to be a purpose in where he was headed… those mountains.

As though guided by a gut instinct, or by the will of the Elders, or maybe his own vanity, he had a feeling that an answer was there, in the distance.

Occasionally he would glance around, but as expected, neither could he see anyone, nor was anything tailing him.

Just like his old friends, he was … alone.

~

JAMIESONN STOOD ON top of the cliff and stared off into the distance across the ocean. He could see into Tanzac's world, and he not only could see the fallen demi-god gloat in his own vanity, but also see Alex and what perils lay ahead.

Jamiesonn knew only too well that Alex wouldn't be able to confront his alter-ego, but then again, he was hardly going to interfere. He wanted Alex dead as much as everyone else did.

He sneered and turned his attention away to focus on what mattered in this world.

"Is it time, father?" He heard a woman speak from behind him.

"Almost. My precious daughter." He replied and looked at his daughter, Laura. Behind her, standing some feet away, were his beloved Hell Vixens. Anxiously awaiting orders from their master.

He smiled at them, almost lustfully. He sensed their hunger for new virgin blood, and that hunger was great.

It was almost a year ago when Laura turned to the darkness, and in that time, she had grown a lot in her powers. She was as beautiful, cunning and seductive as she was evil. Her former life was nothing more than a faded memory, thanks to Jamiesonn.

The life she once had, the fiancée, Garry, even her coworkers… all gone. Even the former Queen of Hell was a faded memory now.

Laura did not remember slaughtering her mother, Cathy, to become the new Queen of Hell. Nor did she remember slaughtering Garry that night that she gave herself to this darkness. The only thing she knew was that she was his queen, and she ruled second only to Jamiesonn.

Laura stepped forward toward the cliff-face and stared off across the ocean.

"The Fallen One is plotting to return, father." She said

"I know." Jamiesonn replied.

"Then we should act before the Fallen One has a chance to unleash his own army upon this world." She said as she turned to look at him.

Jamiesonn smiled evilly, "Daughter, don't be too hasty with your actions. All things take time, and just as it was with the fall of the Elders, so too the destruction of the Fallen One."

Laura looked aside. She knew Jamiesonn was right. She was there to witness Jamiesonn confront the Elders not too long ago. She saw firsthand how powerful the Elders were, but even with their combined power, they could not stand against Jamiesonn.

Even now, the Elders were held captive in Jamiesonn's world, which had become more terrifying than what it already was ever since his *resurrection*.

"Sorry father." She said. She turned away and sighed softly. "What of the Chosen?"

Jamiesonn placed his hand on her shoulder, "His time will come, and you shall bring new meaning to the torment he shall endure."

Laura smiled, relishing that thought.

Jamiesonn turned and walked away towards the cavern entrance. He stopped momentarily to glance over at his vixens and looked back to the cavern.

"Go." He said, "Do what you must and bring me the life of the untouched."

With that, the vixens screeched with pleasure and vanished into smoke to go find their next victim.

Jamiesonn smirked then walked off inside the cavern entrance and vanished, immediately reappearing in his own realm.

Laura stood at the cliff-side for a few moments and turned her gaze to where Alex was. Like her father, she could see what was ahead, and she merely smirked.

"Your end comes… Chosen One." She scoffed before she turned away and immediately vanished.

2

Jamiesonn's resurrection was by no means a case where one day he was incarcerated in his own world, then the next he was free. His escape from captivity came by the Elders themselves.

> *From the Light, the Son of Wrath is released, to set right the ways of the past to bring forth that which shall be - Azullrokr the Prophet 16:22.*
>
> *—Book of Mezunabite. 5,308BC*

From their position, the Elders watched and could see that unless they intervened with Jamiesonn's incarceration, then Tanzac's power would rise and so to would his armies.

Taking it upon themselves, one of the Elders descended into Jamiesonn's world and found him, bound by Alex's power and in insufferable torment.

Jamiesonn saw the old sage from out of the corner of his eye, and could only scream, "What. Do. You. Want. Here. Old. One. To. See. Me. Suffer. More?"

The Elder immediately changed his form from light into human and took a few steps towards him.

"As much as you deserve to suffer for all eternity Dark One, I am here on another purpose."

"Then. What."

"We shall spare your suffering for the end of days, but there is a threat coming to our Chosen."

"And. You. Want. Me. To. Help."

"Rather not, but if you give your blood oath, released you will be."

Jamiesonn screeched in agony as he hung, bound there, and finally he nodded. The Elder looked at him for a long moment then clicked his fingers. At once, Jamiesonn was released from the bonds that held him, and he collapsed, weak, to the ground.

"What is it you expect from me, old man?"

The Elder looked down at him and remarked, "Such a loss, of one who had great potential to be our messenger."

Jamiesonn slowly got to his feet and glared at him, "What is it you want of me?"

The Elder paused for a moment then said, "The Darkness is coming, and this time in greater numbers."

"You mean that fool, Tanzac?" Jamiesonn remarked as he brushed himself off. "Alex incarcerated him… remember?"

"Ah yes. That he was. But we have seen that even now, the Darkness is finding a way back, and Tanzac is amassing an even greater army."

"Let me guess." Jamiesonn remarked, "You want me to stop the armies while that fucker, Alex, plays the hero in all this? What? Just to have my ass in bondage again? Save the sales pitch, old one. Alex did that before and look what that got me!"

The elder stepped up to him and snarled, "Don't play games with us, Dark One. We have seen that Tanzac is becoming more powerful, and since Alex is not yet powerful enough to face the Darkness and his armies, the duty is now upon you to finish it."

Jamiesonn paused, and took a step back.

"Why is it now *upon* me?"

The Elder smirked and remarked, "The only way you get to confront Alex is by making sure Tanzac is out of the way."

"Interesting… But knowing you lot, there is a trap to all this."

The Elder sneered and just stared at him.

Jamiesonn stepped forward, and demanded, "Then it's on my terms!"

"As you wish." The Elder remarked, as he began to walk away.

"Hey!" Jamiesonn yelled, "You don't know what they are!"

"Oh, we are aware of those." The Elder commented, as he gradually vanished.

Jamiesonn looked around, almost afraid for some moments, then before his eyes he watched as his kingdom began to restore into an even more evil glorious kingdom.

Jamiesonn watched and saw what had become of his kingdom. In a matter of moments, the once suffering children were transformed into his Hell Spawn, while some women, were transformed into his seductive Hell Vixens. Even Cathy, the one he loved to hate, had been changed.

Jamiesonn fell on his knees and laughed with insane delight.

～

THE ELDERS MAY have had the best intentions with their plan, but they obviously underestimated Jamiesonn, especially when it came to him having his own ideas of how things should be run.

Jamiesonn had his own agenda, and the only thing that consumed his mind was revenge.

In a short time, Jamiesonn grew more powerful than he once was, but yet, was still beyond the reach of returning to Earth as he was. As limited as he was in his own world, he did know the one way back, and that was through Karen, and her unborn child.

3

KAREN AWOKE WITH a sudden gasp and sat upright in the bed. Her face was covered in a cold sweat and she was trembling. It took her a few moments to compose herself, then she slowly looked over to her right.

Her boyfriend, Jonah, was asleep, snoring, as was the normal thing for him after a night out with the guys.

Karen sat on the edge of the bed and slowly drank the glass of water that was on her bedside table.

"What a fucking nightmare" she muttered softly. "Thank fuck that loser is out of my life." She went on as she got up out of bed and went to the bathroom.

The events of her life were not spectacular to say the least. She remembered her time with Alex which, as she would say to all her girlfriends, was *a fucking disaster waiting to happen.* After her life of living with Alex in Auckland, she moved back to Melbourne to start her life over. But the plans she had for a better life came to no fruition, as she went from one lover to the next, and somewhere along the line of ex- boyfriends that were either druggies, alcoholics and even a pimp, she ended up with Jonah.

Jonah was no one in particular. He worked at a trucking firm in Laverton North. Jonah wasn't the best-looking guy on the block. He stood at about 6 feet 2, weighed about 180 kgs, was balding at the splendid age of 23, was a fan of loop earrings, and talking shit to anyone who cared to listen. Jonah was not the best catch, but to Karen, he mattered to her, as she finally had someone she felt connected to.

Karen washed her face, slipped out of her blue silk nightie and took a shower and prepared for her day. For her that meant tinkering in the backyard with whatever scrap metal was there, cooking homemade chicken strips, walking her Staffy dog and brewing more batches of homemade beer.

Once a week she would trek over to the park a few blocks away to wait for the local food van to show up. Not that she needed food, but, in her estimation, she scored free food for herself and any one of her friends who may happen to show up during the week.

The life she was living was a damn far cry from what she wanted when she was much younger, but for now, it was her life.

Not that Karen was the most prized possession in the world herself. She loathed technology, stayed clear of Facebook unless she was drunk on cheap red wine, and thought that special offers for *free credit cards* and '*win grocery store coupons*' in her email were legitimate offers.

～୨

JONAH (OR LUGNUTS as Karen called him), rose at around 10 am, and after drinking a soft drink, and making small talk to Karen, he got into his Land Rover and headed off to his brother's place in Melton, leaving Karen to get on with her day.

Little did either of them know that Jamiesonn was watching them, waiting for his moment to *shine*.

～୨

"THAT IS CERTAINLY unexpected." Jamiesonn commented, as he watched Karen from his realm. He watched closer, taking note of everything she did, everything that was inside her… especially …

~ാ

As THE DAY played out, Jamiesonn watched and waited for his moment. He knew when he would strike, and that attack would be swift.

~ാ

As WAS HER normal routine, Karen went for her afternoon rest at around 3 pm. It had been a busy morning for her. Preparing food for Jonah, tinkering in the yard, and talking shit with the local bottle shop manager. As she drifted into sleep, little did she know that things would not be the same after today, especially not for her.

4

KAREN AWOKE TO find herself on a long winding gravel road, somewhere in a lush vast valley. Unlike the valley that Alex was in, this was lush and full of rolling green countryside. She could see various livestock wandering around in the near distance, and with them wild beasts such as tigers and lions roaming with them.

"What is this place?" She questioned herself.

At first, she thought she was in some form of heaven, but her reasoning dismissed that immediately as she knew she wouldn't be that fortunate.

In the distance, up over the next bend she could hear some form of celebration going on. She smiled to herself and started to make her way towards those sounds. *"Cool, I'm tonguing for a cold one"* she thought to herself.

$\sim$

AS SHE ROUNDED the bend, she could see a small gathering of people outside of what looked to be a rustic medieval inn, and the people there were also dressed in medieval clothing. From where she stood she could see the people were cheering, drinking ale, and celebrating. She could feel the atmosphere in this place. She sensed a lot of happiness here. But there was also something oddly familiar about what was going on. She looked behind her, seeing only the way she had come, then looked back at the crowd. A part of her wanted to head back the way she had come, but then again, she wanted to go a bit further and not only see what was going on, but join these people.

From where she stood she saw the old inn, and next to it on either side, rustic homes, quite evident of the time. Her impression – or so she thought – was that she had journeyed back to a previous life, and was witnessing an event that she had been a part of.

Deciding to go with her instinct – or her thirst for good beer – she journeyed forth to join them.

"Heyyyy." She almost proclaimed to one of the crowd. "What's going on?"

"Ah wee lassy." One of the men replied. "We be celebrating."

"Oh yeah." She said, "What are we celebrating?"

"Oh, didn't you know?" Another replied.

"Know what?" She smiled

"That being the conception of the deliver." A third man said.

Karen looked at them, almost strangely. "What?"

A random woman slugged over to her and putting a cup of ale in her hand she said, "Come. Let's drink and celebrate."

Karen looked at the tankard of ale in her hand, looked at the middle-aged woman, smiled and decided to go along with this. After all, it was *only* a dream, right?

⁓

KAREN SWIGGED DOWN tankard after tankard of ale with the locals, oblivious to what was going on around her, or more to the point, the shadowy figure that stood nearby, leaning against a wall, and watching these festivities proceed, just as he knew that they would.

He smirked and commented under his breath, "Too easy." He watched, with delight, as she continued to drink and drink and drink more, well into the night. She did not understand what exactly they were celebrating, nor did she really care. All she knew was that she was having a good time drinking and loudly sharing her own stories of her failed and deprived childhood with these people. Stories of how she was deprived of toys, how she was moved around a lot and of course, how an ex-boyfriend raped her and her dog one night, then hung himself in the house next door.

Not that the locals cared, as they were all part of this scheme. This plan to bring her undone.

Karen drank herself to the point of falling over, and when she was done, she passed out on the floor. Not knowing, or caring, where she was.

The shadowy figure finally came out of the darkness and walked over to her. Kneeling down, he outstretched his hand and touched her stomach.

"Now." He said, "Carry me to the new world."

With that, he immediately vanished.

5

KAREN AWOKE SOME time later, groggy and feeling very sick. She sat slowly up in bed and looked around. The clock read 11.57 pm, and instinctively she looked beside her to see that Jonah was not there.

"Cunt." She muttered, as she slowly got up out of bed and staggered to the kitchen. As she poured herself a coffee, all she could think about was that dream she had. That strange dream. If it was only a dream, why the hell did she feel hung over?

She almost grunted and sat at the table and drank her strong coffee.

"Fuck." She cursed. Again, she took another sip of coffee, and with that sip, she started to be hit with severe cramps in her lower stomach. Karen clutched her stomach and slowly started to stand. The pain in her stomach started to get more severe with each passing moment. This was worse than the time she had morning sickness, or the time she aborted the baby to her father.

She struggled to the bathroom to throw up, but before she could get there, she started vomiting blood all over the kitchen floor. In desperation, she grabbed her phone from the counter and called Jonah, hoping to hell he would answer.

As he answered after several rings, all she could whimper was "help" before she collapsed on the floor unconscious.

~

SHE CAME TO, in a hospital bed, dazed and unknowing what exactly happened. Karen glanced around to see a nurse beside her bed, and Jonah standing at the end of the bed.

"What happened?" She asked, groggily.

"You almost had a miscarriage." Jonah said.

"What the fuck?" She asked. "But I'm not pregnant." She tried to sit up.

The nurse insisted she lay down again.

"I don't think you know Miss, but you are pregnant."

"What?" She said, rubbing her head. This was not making sense at all.

"Thankfully your partner got you here in time, otherwise you would have lost the baby."

"But I'm not pregnant!" She insisted.

"I have to tell you, you are. Four months to be exact." The nurse stated.

"What the fuck?" She muttered in disbelief, then looked at Jonah.

"Hey, don't blame me. I'm sterile, remember!" He almost laughed.

"Karen," The nurse spoke, "It's best you rest now. We can talk more tomorrow."

Karen lay back down, and holding her hand on her head, she could only hope that this was nothing more than a fucking dream.

~

"FEELING BETTER TODAY?" The nurse asked, as Karen started to wake.

"Nothing a wine won't fix." She remarked, as she sat up.

"Probably not a good idea, considering." She replied.

"Considering?"

"Yes. Considering you're four months pregnant, and any alcohol could affect the development of your baby."

"Fuck off." Karen muttered, "I can't be…" She sat forward and took a good look around the room. She could see that she was in a hospital room, but just to make sure she wasn't dreaming, she pinched herself hard.

"OUCH!"

Nope. She was indeed awake.

"How'd I get here?" she asked the nurse.

"Oh, your friend brought you in last night." She answered, "But we'd like to keep you here a day or two to run some tests, to make sure everything is okay."

Karen sighed heavily. Having a baby is the last thing she wanted, especially at this point in her life. As much as this wasn't her choice to have a baby, it seemed that the powers that be had other ideas.

~

SOMETIME LATER, AN orderly entered the room with a wheelchair, and took her down to an examination room. Karen still felt out of place here, but there was nothing she could do. Not that she was in a rush to leave. She was quite enjoying being doted over for a change. Instead of Jonah coming over every other night for cheap-thrill sex, and for someone who was supposed to be sterile, he sure as fuck managed to get her pregnant… or did he?

As she was placed on the examination table, she began to fear the worst. Was the baby okay?

Maybe it's time to make changes in my life, she thought as she was prepared for the ultrasound.

She felt nervous, scared, and profoundly, very much alone.

Alex. She thought instinctively, as she looked away from the monitor and a tear escaped her eye.

"Ah. This can't be right." The nurse almost exclaimed.

Karen turned her attention to the here and now and looked at the nurse with grave concern.

"What can't be right?" She almost demanded.

"Ah, wait. Please." The nurse said as she got up and hurried out of the room.　　　　　　　\

Karen sat up and looked out of the room. "For fucks sake." She muttered. "No fucking clue these people."

She slumped back on the bed and sighed, wearily. By now she had enough of being here, and wanted to leave.

But the powers that be had other plans!

~

A FEW MOMENTS later the nurse and another doctor rushed into the room.

"Hey! What the fuck is going on!" Karen demanded.

"It's okay Miss. Just relax so we can see what's going on. The important thing is not to get yourself stressed!"

"Stressed?" She retorted, "Seems to be the only ones here who are causing stress are you people!"

"Please!" the nurse insisted, "Just relax so we can see what's wrong."

Much to her dislike, Karen laid back, and looked away. She didn't want to be here, that was obvious. She didn't want any part of this… charade… She wanted to be home with her lesbian dog and her idiot on-again, off-again boyfriend… but that was not meant to be, at least, not today. She wanted to protest, but that she could reserve for another time, probably the next time she was drunk.

~

"DOCTOR, CAN YOU look at this." The nurse said. The doctor who was with her leaned in for a closer look, then removed his glasses and took another look.

"This is definitely not right." He commented.

"What now?' She remarked. She didn't notice how her stomach had increased in size, as once again, she was focused on herself. Or more to the point, the supposed incompetence of others.

The doctor and nurse both looked at each other, dismayed, then looked at Karen. They had no idea what to say about what they saw before. Karen glanced over to the Ultrasound monitor, and gasped with shock to see, before her eyes the baby grow before her eyes.

"What the fuck??" She gasped, as she witnessed a tiny flash of light on the monitor and a second later, her baby had grown in size. Karen looked at the doctor, then at her stomach. Right before their eyes, her stomach grew before everyone's eyes, starting to bring her to full term.

Karen began screaming in agony. "Please, get this fucking thing out of me!"

The doctor and nurse were dumbfounded.

"Get her to the maternity ward!" The doctor screamed, almost hysterically.

Immediately the nurse ran out of the room, screaming, terrified, to find help.

Soon I will be reborn, and with me the darkness comes. A voice echoed in the halls.

> *In the days of the last, the Son of Perdition will come from her belly, and the Darkness shall be unleashed to consume the inhabitants from Melshaiah to Gaohakioran*
>
> —*Azullrokr the Prophet.*

Karen screamed in horrific pain as she was taken to the maternity ward, and all she could scream for was Jonah. Yet, he was nowhere to be reached. His cell phone gave off a disconnected signal, and everyone that was tried to be called by one of the nurses, the same thing. All numbers were busy or disconnected!

Karen was rushed into the maternity ward, and the doctors began to operate on her. Only a C-section could save her life at this point.

Karen slumped on the hospital bed, weary, exhausted, and absolutely fed-up. With each passing minute, her birth pains grew in intensity, and she knew within herself that she would survive.

If only.... If only, Alex were here.

But he wasn't! He was in never-never land dealing with his own shit!

~

AFTER THE DOCTOR gave her an epidural, they started the procedure to deliver the baby. With each passing minute though, the baby continued to grow in size, until the point where it was full term and ready to come into the world.

The doctors did everything they could to fight against the clock to make sure both the baby and mother were alive, but time was not on their side.

As they operated, they could see on the monitor that for some unknown and unheard of reason, the baby had already broken out of his sac and started to devour the insides of his mother, starting with her heart. Blood began to spurt out of her chest, then her mouth and nose. She screamed in agonizing pain and begged the doctors to get the baby out of her.

For a few seconds, there was chaos in the delivery room from what they were seeing, until one of the nurses put an oxygen mask on Karen, to try and keep her alive, but it was futile. A moment later, they all heard the distinct cracking of bones, and after that, they stood back and watched in shock as her rib-cage broke open and blood began to erupt out of her exposed chest like a fountain of blood.

"Get the baby out!" The head doctor, doctor Tsuikiusk exclaimed in almost broken English.

Fervently, they fought harder, to try and save the baby. At least, at this point, the baby could be saved.

With a final cut, a final incision, they delivered the baby, but it was too late. With a final breath, Karen died in an agonizing scream, leaving the baby in the arm of the doctor who delivered him.

"It's a boy." He merely stated, saddened, and looked at the dead mother.

With such innocence of a new-born, the child looked up at the doctor and smiled. Innocence was all he could see in the baby's eyes, but he knew something darker was at work behind all this. All the doctor could do was look at the baby, then look at the others in the operating room. As much as they could try to save Karen, they couldn't.

The doctor sighed heavily. He had seen a few situations like this in his thirty-year career, but nothing was ever like this. In his thirty years of being a doctor – both in his homeland, and here in Melbourne – he had delivered numerous babies, and seen a few occurrences where the mother died in child-birth. But this? He had never seen the likes of this!

Doctor Tsuikiusk handed the baby to the maternity nurse, and she slowly walked out of the room.

No one knew what the fuck happened, but one thing was for sure. Doctor Tsuikiusk knew that the child needed to be protected.

6

IN THE WEEKS that followed Karen's death, Doctor Tsuikiusk adopted the child, legally, through the connections he had already made through the DHS. He knew that there was something astounding about the child, and with the help of his connections in the DHS – and some bribe cash – he managed to secure the legal adoption of the child. Majeed Tsuikiusk was a firm believer in Islam faith, and he held sacred his religion and his own Iraqi cultural background. He already had sons of his own, back in Iraq, and as promising as they were, their esteem was small in comparison to his adopted son.

Majeed came from a wealthy family in the post-Iraqi war, and he immigrated to Melbourne in the 1990's. He was a doctor in Iraq, and thanks to much red-tape cutting, he was able to carry on his profession in Melbourne.

It didn't take long for Majeed to take on a doctor role at one of the hospitals in Melbourne, and soon after, he was able to buy a house in Melbourne's Eastern suburbs, Bentley, and he was soon able to hire housekeepers and a gardener. A family, in fact, from Indonesia.

By the time the child was born, the family from Indonesia had already been working for Majeed for almost 20 years.

After the birth of the child, Tsuikiusk took the child as his ward of the state and entrusted him to his housekeepers, Arthur, Astuti and their daughter, Patricia who were charged with taking care of the male child – whom he named Akram.

Little did any of them know that the child, Akram, was not who he appeared to be... At least, not to help the employees of Majeed.

~

LIKE ANY OTHER day in the Tsuikiusk household. Doctor Majeed arrived home at the usual time of 6.00 pm. After he opened the remote gate, and drove through to the garage, he gave his BMW M3 a final look over and proceeded into the house.

As he expected to see, the house was spotlessly clean, as it was any other day. But this day was different for some reason. No, this day, there was something amiss.

Majeed placed his keys down on the hall table and glanced around.

"Akram!" He called out... No answer. "Arthur! Astuti!" he paused, then went on, "Tish?"

Again, no answer.

"AKRAM!" He yelled as loud as he could. For a moment there was silence, then, from upstairs, he heard the sound of footsteps, slowly making their way down the hall.

"Akram!" Majeed exclaimed, looking up at his son, who was now visibly a teenager, "What have you done??"

Akram merely looked down at him. His trusted guardian, and said, "Akram."

Majeed glared at him and could only stumble back and say,

"What are you?... What did you do to...?"

"The help?" Was the answer, as he started to walk slowly down the stairs "Oh, don't worry about them. They'll be no trouble now, since their days of their stealing has ended, Father."

"What have you done?" Majeed said softly, fearful, as he stumbled and fell on the floor. "Wh-what are you?"

Akram jumped forward, like any arrogant teenager would do in a similar situation of dominance or power, and threw his hand in the air.

"Don't you remember me, Father!" He yelled. "Not long ago, you delivered me into this world from that whore-fuck, Karen... if you remember!"

"No..." Majeed muttered, as he scurried backwards on the floor until he was back up against the front door.

"Wh-what are you?" he again muttered, as his adopted son stormed towards him.

"What?" He answered, almost quizzically, "You don't know me??" He shrugged his shoulders and almost protested. "You don't know the one child you fucking saved from that scum, Karen? You don't know the child whom you gave some fucking idiot name to? Seriously??"

With that, he grabbed Majeed by the scruff of the neck and tossed him effortlessly across the room.

"Son. Why are you d-d-doing this?" Majeed said, weakly.

"Son? Son?" Came the reply, as he stormed toward him. "I am not anyone's begotten son, yours or otherwise."

With that, he grabbed Majeed again and threw him through the glass door that went into the dining room. Akram stormed into the room and grabbed his adopted father by the throat and began to strangle the very life out of him.

"W-Wh-Wha.." Was the only thing that Majeed could struggle to say.

Akram pulled him close to his face, glared at him with intense hatred and then snuffed.

"Your house slaves I killed." He muttered. "Their blood and intestines paint my walls, and the stench of their torment will ascend for a thousand generations."

"Wh-why?" Majeed chocked out

Akram pulled him close enough to lick his face, then pushed him back enough to look into his eyes.

"Do you know who I am?" he said.

Majeed could barely shake his head. But Akram leaned in closer and whispered,

"I am the one foretold by all the ancient texts. I am that which was, is, and will be. I am the Son of the Dark…." He paused just for a moment, then went on… "Call … me … Jamiesonn."

With that, he snapped his neck, then slowly rose to his feet and breathed in the new scent of this death. The new smell of death was very satisfying to his being. Even more so than the Indonesians he murdered not less than thirty minutes ago.

Jamiesonn looked around the house. He knew there would be nothing of interest here. After all, he had spent all of the last 3 months growing up here… not years… in three months he had grown from a new born baby to a fully-grown adult.

Despite what science, physics, and religion may have said, Jamiesonn was of another breed entirely. And now that he was resurrected, he was far more powerful than the Elders, and maybe even more so than Tanzac.

But… Before he could do anything, he knew he had things to do before he could destroy the Chosen One… That was, to bring about the rise of his daughter, go back to stop Tanzac from destroying the ancient world, free Alex from the world he was currently in, destroy the Elders, and then stop somewhere to have pancakes for breakfast.

Jamiesonn looked at the current world… a population of almost eight billion people, and he smirked evilly. He knew that there was nothing to stop him from being the dominant ruler of the world. But yet, that thorn in his fucking side… Alex… was always there.

Jamiesonn huffed heavily and looked around at the carnage he had already created. He took pride in the murders he committed, but that wasn't enough. He wanted more, and the only way he would get more is by the resurrection of Alex.

He knew damn well, that once the Chosen was resurrected and in full steam, would he be able to do his take-over of the world… free or otherwise.

Jamiesonn took one final look at the house he had grown to

somewhat tolerate over the last few months, took final delight in the murders he had committed, before he walked out the front door and vanished into the darkness of the night.

7

In a twinkling of an eye, Jamiesonn reappeared in the ancient throne room of Tanzac. Immediately he knew where he was. In the room of the Ancients... The birthplace of his forefathers.

He looked around the room, staring at the scene before him. He could hear the screams of terror, fear of the tribes of this land, and as much as he wanted to take delight in the massacre of these people and their destruction, he knew that if he stood by and did nothing, he would only be adding to the cause of this vile entity Tanzac.

Seeing the suffering brought him a great sense of euphoria, to see these mortals in torment, but his own future depended on their existence.

Jamiesonn glanced around the room, and saw his target. Tanzac stood there in all his unholy glory, ready to strike any mortal – or anyone – who dared to stand in his way.

"How..." Jamiesonn began, "Has the fallen become full of pride."

Tanzac turned and his eyes widened in surprise when he saw the tall man standing nearby. Jamiesonn's eyes shone brilliantly blue. Tanzac sensed power in him and knew that his power was far greater than what he had sensed in Alex.

"You possess great power mortal," Tanzac remarked.

"Yes, I do. It's a shame you will not be around to see my rise," he replied coldly.

Tanzac frowned and sneered at him. "Who do you think you are! A mere—"

"Call me Master," Jamiesonn interrupted. "Now it is time for your species to face the first wrath." He raised one hand, and immediately Tanzac was struck in the chest by an unseen force.

The blow was powerful enough to make this mighty fallen god stumble backwards a few feet. It took Tanzac by surprise, and for a moment he wondered just where this man could have gotten such great power. Tanzac stood upright and snarled at him, this stranger who possessed greater power than he had ever seen from any mortal before. Yet, he also knew the power was dark and evil, just like his own, and somehow that made him feel a touch of pride.

Tanzac unleashed his own attack, but Jamiesonn had expected it and defended against it easily. Tanzac unleashed more powerful blows in succession, but each attack was to no avail. It was as though Jamiesonn knew exactly what Tanzac was going to do before he did it.

"Enough of this," Jamiesonn remarked. "I have had enough of playing this charade with you, Tanzac!"

Tanzac was struck powerfully in the chest. This time the blow found its target, and the mighty beast stumbled to his knees, howling in pain.

The screeching howls of Tanzac could be heard from far and wide, and within moments, Lutancix appeared next to his master, to aid him in his assault against this *newcomer*.

Lutancix let out a loud shriek and lunged at Jamiesonn, but it seemed that Jamiesonn had expected this, and at once he raised his hand, sending Lutancix flying across the room and landing hard, head-first into one of the pillars. Lutancix shook his oversized head and snarled, then took one glance towards his master and scurried off into the dark part of the room, behind a series of pillars.

Before Tanzac had the chance to get out of the way, he was engulfed in an invisible field and sent crashing on his back on the ground.

"Foolish creature," Jamiesonn said as he walked over and knelt down near him. "It is unwise to fight one you cannot destroy. I am the beginning and the fucking end."

"Mortal," Tanzac began. "If only you—" He stopped suddenly when he heard the distinct sound of croaking from nearby. He looked out of the corner of his eye and couldn't see anyone, but he knew Lutancix was there. He smirked wickedly at his situation.

"I hear you, oh Lutancix. Come out from hiding so you can suffer the same fate as your master," Jamiesonn said, not bothering to stand up.

Croaking! He heard that croaking again, and before Jamiesonn had a chance to speak another word, Lutancix let out an ear-piercing screech from nearby and flew towards them. Jamiesonn turned his head quickly and immediately a force struck the great demon and sent him flying off the balcony.

Lutancix landed on his face on the street below. For the first time since his own fall, he felt real pain. As much as he tried to stand, all he could do was crawl towards the vortex. He glanced up towards the top of the temple and shuddered fearfully snarling. "Another time, mortal," he said coldly as he crawled back into the vortex.

"Thanks to your kind," Jamiesonn said, looking back at Tanzac, "I was resurrected from the ashes of my own incarceration, and now I have come to restore what was rightfully mine."

"You are fucking with the wrong powers!" Tanzac snarled.

"I don't think so!" he replied. "But I guess I should be saying thanks anyway. After all, you gave me the power to become what I am now."

Tanzac glared up at him. "And who are you?"

Jamiesonn looked closer at the fallen demi-god and remarked, "In time, you will call me by name... Jamiesonn. You took what was mine from me twice. There shall not be a third time."

"I take... whatsoever I choose!" Tanzac screamed.

Not any more, old one." Jamiesonn replied. "The prophecy has become mine to fulfill, as you will discover in time to come!"

"I will remember this!"

"No... You won't. You and your kind will not even remember I was here." Jamiesonn rose to his feet and glared at the demon of old. "The first wrath comes!" he said as he took a step back.

Jamiesonn knew what he had to do. He watched Tanzac struggle desperately to break free of his invisible prison, but fail. The power, whatever it was, was even more powerful than he was. Jamiesonn could only smirk evilly.

Jamiesonn raised his finger, and Tanzac was hoisted off the ground effortlessly by an invisible force. He hovered in mid-air, as though he was to become a sacrifice himself.

"You may have been able to kill the One, but you sure as fuck will never destroy me, sooka!" Jamiesonn scoffed.

"We shall see, mortal!" Tanzac snarled in return.

Jamiesonn sneered. With a slight twitch of his forefinger, Tanzac was sent soaring off the balcony, screaming furiously as he was sent flying into the vortex.

At once, his horde of demons ceased their attack and turned their attention towards the temple. They could sense Jamiesonn and his great power, and they all immediately feared him. They ceased their massacre and fled at once, back into the vortex.

Jamiesonn watched them fleeing back into the vortex, back to the only place they were safe: Tanzac's realm. The demons may have had power to torture and murder vast numbers of mortals, but they could only do what their Master ordered. Just as Jamiesonn had promised Tanzac, as each one entered the vortex, not one of them remembered Jamiesonn ever being here.

As far as they all knew, Alex was the one who incarcerated them in that place.

When the last of the demons had fled, Jamiesonn looked down at the vortex and focused his power to close the doorway, making it impossible for any of the powerful demons within to create havoc in this time. The vortex stopped spinning and, within seconds, it had vanished. With it, the darkness also began to recede. The dark clouds rolled back just as rapidly as they had appeared, and Jamiesonn saw that the eclipse was now over.

Jamiesonn rested his hands on the stone rail of the balcony. "Okay, Alex," he muttered. "I fulfilled your prophecy".

Now it's time to fulfill mine." He paused for a moment and smirked. "Fuck, it's great to be back."

He walked back inside and went over to Azullrokr and Nanomi. For a second, the thought crossed his mind to sever their heads and drink their blood, but he ignored the urge. He crouched down in front of them and looked at them. They were both still unconscious, which may have been a good thing. He glanced first at Azullrokr and then stared at Nanomi for a longer time. He saw how beautiful she was, but he was not in the least bit interested in her.

"Now I see why Alex loved you," he whispered. "Just as in time you will give yourself for him."

He waved his hand over them, and they woke up with a startle.

"Oh!" Azullrokr said, quickly looking around, 'What happened?"

"The one who betrayed you has been dealt with," Jamiesonn said as he rose to his feet.

They looked up at him, and who they saw was Alex – not Jamiesonn.

"Oh, thank you," Nanomi said as he helped her to her feet. "How could we have been so blind?" Azullrokr said.

"What can we do to thank you?"

"Nothing," Jamiesonn said. "I was only here to fulfil prophecy. Now I must go, and your people must continue to survive."

Jamiesonn would have loved nothing better than to kill these people himself. That was his nature, and his only passion. But he was here for a reason: to fulfill the prophecy. And he knew very well that if he slaughtered these people himself, he would never exist.

Alex may well have been the last of the bloodline, but in another time, so was Jamiesonn. Jamiesonn too, was a descendant of these people. He knew it. He and Alex were more closely related than he liked. He glanced around one last time. Using his power, he could see that only a small handful of the people of the village had survived the massacre. "Well what do ya know," he muttered. "Prophecy does come full circle after all."

He took one last glance at Azullrokr and Nanomi before he vanished, returning to where he had come from to fulfill his own dark prophecy.

In time to come, the real Alex would once again be united to Nanomi. But not yet. That was for a time to come. When the prophecy was aligned.

8

Jamiesonn looked and watched Laura from the distance, as she got off the bus and walked to her work-place. She was fragile, still grieving over the loss of Tony…

Alas, poor Tony. Just a waste… Such a tool.

Jamiesonn knew that she was ripe for his picking. She was insecure… easy prey for this dark master.

Jamiesonn could have his way with any person, any woman. But, this was not his will. Not yet. He wanted this one. He wanted Laura… He needed her.

~

Jamiesonn had a plethora of mind-games at his disposal. He could use any method he wanted to break her, and that he did.

Turning Laura to his side, to see who she really was, was a feat easier than expected. All it took was the right mind games and the use of that idiot, Garry.

From that night, Jamiesonn knew that he was finally unstoppable, and his lovely daughter was not so ordinary as some thought.

Jamiesonn's time was coming, and he had the Chosen One to face, but now that he finally had his daughter, Laura, by his side, he intended to have fun with the mortals first. First stop for him was a mass killing spree to liven up his own party, and make the world know exactly who he was.

Finally... He would get to rule this disgusting, filthy planet, and all those who lived he would make them fear the very sound of his name.

Jamiesonn vanished from Laura's presence, and started on his own agenda, while his Vixens accompanied Laura to her new home... In Hell.

9

ALEX ENTERED THE cavern. It was dark and surprisingly cold. There was a flicker of light off in the distance, like a campfire. He hesitated for a moment. He sensed danger ahead, but that feeling he pushed aside just as fast as it came.

"No time to get paranoid now," He muttered. "Go on I must."

Alex made his way through the wide cavern, heading gradually towards that light. He knew someone was here. That much was obvious. And he just hoped to hell that it wasn't his alter ego.

His own questioning didn't have long to wait, as no sooner had he gotten closer, he heard a cracking noise behind him.

Quickly he turned around, but saw no one.

"Dammit." He whispered, then he turned back towards the fire up ahead.

"Miss me bitch." His alter ego snarled, then hit him hard in the face.

Alex fell on his back, stunned by the sheer force with which his alter ego hit him.

"You... again." He said as he stumbled slowly to his feet.

His alter ego said nothing. Just glared intently at him with sheer hatred and stormed towards him. Again, Alex was punched with intense force and sent crashing against the cavern wall, some distance behind him.

For some moments, Alex couldn't move. He groaned and almost wanted to cry. He was in pain, a lot of pain. The nerve endings in his back spasmed, and his only thought was that he was paralysed.

He wasn't.

He knew that he was no real match for this creature, and part of him wanted to die. Alex had done his part for King and Country. He had stopped the Darkness before in Winmont, and that should have been it for him. But no. Here he was, to face this creature in this god-forsaken hell, with hardly any of his supernatural abilities.

If only he hadn't walked away from his calling… if only he hadn't shacked up with Karen … if only.

"Get up!" His alter ego screeched, as he kicked Alex in the chest.

SNAP!

The sound of bones breaking echoed.

His ribs were broken. Alex howled in agonizing pain and he started to weep.

His enemy smirked and laughed, at the fate of this once great *Chosen One*.

"Now.. You end." He snarled.

"Finish it." Alex could only whimper.

With a lunge, his alter ego went to strike his final blow. One final blow and the Chosen One would be dead, and Tanzac would be free to wipe out humanity.

He grabbed Alex and dragged him to his head and grabbed him in a headlock. Alex struggled, but he couldn't escape.

"Hear that?." His enemy snarled, "No heroics here boy. No one to save you. The Master has won."

⁓

WITH ONE SWIFT move, he snapped Alex's neck, and Alex's lifeless body collapsed to the ground.

The creature glared at the dead body, and felt a strong sense of pride, knowing that he alone had killed the last of the bloodline of a forgotten race.

"Master.." He said, "It is done."

He took a final look at the body and turned to walk away.

FROM THE MOMENT that he turned to walk away, a split second later, a person appeared in the cavern, just near Alex's dead body. The creature stopped and turned his head slightly. He sensed something, a power that he hadn't sensed before.

Out of the corner of his eye, he saw the dark man, and he turned to face him.

"You." He commented.

Jamiesonn looked at the creature, then looked down at Alex.

"You don't think that your kind can take that which is my birth-right." He stated.

The creature snarled, "The Master does what he pleases!"

"Pfft."

At once, the creature screeched and lunged towards him, determined to deliver the same fate to him, as he had done to Alex. Jamiesonn raised one hand and clicked his finger. The creature froze in mid-air, then a moment later his body exploded into dust.

"All too easy." He remarked with a smug look on his face. He turned his gaze to Alex and knelt to look closer at him.

"Such a poor ending for the mortal." He quipped, "But you will not die today."

With that he placed one hand on Alex's head and immediately Alex started to stir. He was alive... again.

~

Alex woke with a heavy gasp and looked around quickly, then at Jamiesonn.

"You?" He spoke softly, "Why did you…"

"You already know why Alex." Jamieson said.

Alex glanced around quickly, and seeing they were alone, he could only wonder what the fuck happened.

"You should know better than to interfere with what should be." Alex said as he slowly started to stand.

"That in itself is a contradiction, considering how many times you have interfered with the past. Besides, you know that I will never share my glory with Tanzac."

"Hmm. And you want the glory of killing me yourself, right."

Jamiesonn smirked, "You know that much is right."

Alex sighed and looked away. He knew Jamiesonn spoke the truth, and he knew that if Tanzac won all this, the reign of fire and brimstone would engulf humanity. But then again, the same fate awaited the world if Jamiesonn won.

Looking at his own ending meant that either way, he was fucked.

"Better go do what you must while I regather my power." Alex muttered.

"I will be seeing you soon kid." Jamiesonn said, then vanished

"I can't fucking wait." Alex muttered, once he knew Jamiesonn was gone.

Alex hated this. But right now, there was nothing he could do. All he wanted right now was the balance to be restored and do everything he could to regain his powers.

Right now, that was all that mattered.

He took a glance around this cavern, closed his eyes and focused to try and teleport out of there. He couldn't. He opened his eyes and peered around, hoping to hell he had left here.

No. He was still there.

"Fuck this."

He closed his eyes again and focused harder.

No place like home. He was very tempted to recite over and over. But he didn't. he just groaned heavily and focused on another place, any other place to be right now.

Anywhere was better than here.

"Come on…" He whispered

He strained ….

What seemed to be an eternity later, he vanished from this dark realm.

10

FROM THE TIME of his re-birth to now, Jamiesonns' powers had grown to the point where he was as powerful as a demi-god, probably even more so than Tanzac. Even before in his past life, the power he had was nothing compared to what he had now, and that made him feel damn good about himself.

Jamiesonn reappeared in the very heart of Tanzac's world, in the throne room of the fallen god.

He looked around and smugly sneered at the surroundings. It was dark, dismal, somewhat decayed and smelled like rotting flesh.

"I see you made it here Jamiesonn." He heard Tanzac say from nearby. "I am most impressed to see what you did with my assassin, but raising the dead one you should not have done."

Jamiesonn turned his gaze to Tanzac. He was just as he remembered him, and he remembered that it was not that long ago when he made this fallen god fall on his knees.

"I told you before old one. I take what is mine." Jamiesonn said.

Tanzac stood up from his throne and stepped forward. With just a thought, his generals and lieutenants appeared in the room, behind Jamiesonn, just far back enough to prevent any escape. Jamiesonn sensed Tanzac's demons, and he smirked.

"An army." Jamiesonn sneered, "Not surprising that you would get *the help* to fight your battle. Unlike you, I don't need others to fight my war."

Tanzac growled and waved his mighty arm at his legion.

"He's mine!" He ordered. At once, this legion of protection stood back and watched as their master of ages stepped forward towards Jamiesonn a few feet.

Jamiesonn sized up his opponent, then glanced back at the legion. He could see and sense that there were hundreds of them, laying in wait to watch their master defeat him.

He smirked at the situation and looked back at Tanzac.

Tanzac stood poised. Overbearing in height, overwhelming in strength.

~

FOR MILLENNIA, TANZAC was a god. Ever since the era when his legion was first cast out of Paradise by the archangels, he had been in a war against humanity, and at every opportunity he made sure that the Creators' favorite was made to look like the vile scum that they were.

Tanzac had no desire to return to the Paradise of the Gods. He liked the mortal world far too much, and just as he did in the days of the Mezunabites, he wanted to rule the mortals again and finish what he had begun… Complete chaos.

~

ALEX HAD REAPPEARED, but not where he wanted to be.

He was in a forest, one that was very familiar to him. He looked at himself and he could see that he was wearing his old dark cloak he had in a previous life. He sighed, knowing exactly where he was. He was near the campgrounds where his parents used to come in his childhood.

"Dammit." He muttered. He knew why he was here. To prevent one of his former selves from making another fuck up.

He clenched his fists, and for the first time in what seemed to be an era, he felt power – real power – coursing through his veins.

Somehow that trip to the past started to restore his abilities and strengths, and he liked it. No, he fucking loved it.

He took a deep breath and looked around. He remembered this place too well. Not only from his childhood, but also when he was here some time ago, when his former self confronted his parents.

He looked around slowly. He knew why he was here and what he had to do. He watched, and then saw him headed towards a cabin that was nearby.

"Alex!" He called out. His former self stopped and turned quickly. He couldn't see this new version of himself standing there, and he walked off.

"Don't do it, kid!" he called out again. Once again, his other self stopped and looked around, and turned back to go on ahead.

Dammit Alex. He thought, as he glared at him. Was I ever this *hard-headed.*

Alex vanished and instantly reappeared behind his other self.

"I know what you're intending to do, kid." He said sternly.

His other self froze, fearfully and glanced around slowly.

"Don't be alarmed."

His other self turned slowly and seeing him, was taken aback for a moment. "What are you supposed to be? Some kind of Druid or Sith?"

He ignored his remark, and replied, "I know what you're intending to do. Do you really think that revealing yourself to *her* will change anything?"

"Maybe." He replied quickly, "What would you know anyway?"

"You cannot change what is to come, Alex." He said. "Her fate is sealed, just as you know it is. Telling her of events that are yet to unfold will not save her."

"She's my mother!" His other self yelled, and turned to run off.

Before he could get away, Alex grabbed him by the arm, and pushed him to the ground.

"Don't be an idiot." Alex said, "Think about your actions carefully. If you follow this course of action to the end, it will not end well for you. And those you love will have died for nothing."

His other self could only glare at him for some moments before he spat out, "You would do the same thing if you were me." With that, he scrambled to his feet and ran off.

Alex didn't bother to chase him. He just watched and replied softly, "I know I would. I already did."

Alex stood there for a moment, just watching, then started to trail his other self. He knew that he needed to warn him. But he also remembered vividly how this played out. No matter what he did, history, his own history, was playing out before him like some kind of demented movie where he was one of the lead characters. That, or his life was an episode on the old TV series, The Twilight Zone.

Alex – his other self – stood near the forest clearing and looked around. Ahead of him was his parents cabin.

He was about to step out to continue on his mission, when Alex yelled out to him again.

His other self turned to see the hooded person standing before him.

"Don't be foolish." Alex said.

"How would you know what I am going to do? You don't know me, so take a hike!"

"Always the stubborn one," Alex said, "You get that from your father."

His other self shoved him with force, making him momentarily lose his balance.

Shit! Shoulda remembered that. Alex thought. "Alex!" He snapped, "I know you better than you think. If you reveal yourself to these people, it will destroy everything you will do in the years to come."

"Oh yeah? And why should I even think this place is real?" he retorted. "For all I know, this could be just another damn dream, and you are nothing but the mist of a voice, long since gone."

"Alex, this … this place is real. You are really in this era of time. Why, I cannot tell you, but you must be mindful of your actions. Whatever you do will have serious implications on your own life."

Alex sensed that somehow, the words he was saying were getting through to his other self, or at least, that is what he hoped.

"You do not remember now," Alex said. "But in time everything will be revealed."

"You said that before."

Always the hard way. Alex thought. He knew that he could talk to this version of himself until he was blue in the face, and that would prove as useful as talking to a brick wall.

Alex placed his hand on his shoulder and continued, "Be mindful of the things you do, for soon you will know the truth." With that, he took a step back and vanished.

ALEX COULD REMEMBER how that scenario played out, and as much as he wanted to interfere, he knew that he could not. If he did, then he would not be able to be here now. Wherever *here* was.

He appeared in what looked to be a temple of sorts. In a dimly lit room to be precise. In each corner of the room he could see torches hanging on the wall, each holder made of refined gold, and encrusted with fine jewels on the handles.

On each of the walls, he could see hieroglyphs, each depicting the history of this era. It occurred to him where he was.

"The Mezunabites." He whispered, then said "Nanomi."

He didn't know exactly what era he had teleported to, but he was here for a reason. He just had no clue what that reason was.

He walked towards the hall nearby, knowing where it would lead.

As he walked down the narrow hall, he could hear someone talking up ahead. It was a woman's voice, and at first thought, he expected to know who it was. It was obvious she wasn't alone, as he could hear another voice speaking, a man's. He stopped momentarily to listen more intently, but he couldn't make out what they were saying. He closed his eyes, and focused his power to eavesdrop. Again, he couldn't make out clearly what they were saying. It was as though he was not meant to know what was going on.

He opened his eyes and huffed. He wasn't impressed. He hesitated, then walked on further, with each step the sounds of the conversation becoming more distant. He paused for a moment, just to glance the way he had come, then turned back to peer ahead into the dimness of the hall. He knew there was an exit to another room up ahead; but, part of him wanted to turn away and leave.

Ahead. He muttered. *No point stopping now.*

He hurried ahead, then started to jog, then run. He could hear them talking far ahead, then it became a heated argument. Faster he ran, needing to get to the room up ahead.

Then silence.

The conversation ceased, and Alex stopped in his tracks. Nothing could be heard now, apart from the eerie sound of the faint wind which blew in this hall.

Fuck this. He thought. *This is absolute fucking bullshit.*

As quiet as it was, there was someone in that room up ahead. He knew it. He could sense it.

"Okay, let's get this over with." He muttered and walked off, determined.

Alex walked briskly down the hall. He remembered being here once before, but this time, it seemed to be a longer hike than what it was previously. He didn't like this, not one bit. To him, it felt like a trap. He wished that he could be back somewhere else, anywhere, just for a moment. To a time when things were simpler... even to that time when...

HE ENTERED THE room and instantly, he was in another time and place. He looked around, and seeing that he was in an apartment, he knew where he was.

"Alison." He muttered softly, knowing he was in Alison's apartment. "This can't be right." He said.

Alison had been dead a long time. But, here he was. In her apartment. He took a look around her apartment. She wasn't here, but her smell sure was. How he remembered that smell so vividly. Being one for scented candles, her place always smelled of vanilla, which he always used to love. He walked into the lounge to have a better look around. Against one wall he saw the large screen TV and Sega Saturn he had bought only weeks before, and on the other side of the room, that tacky lounge he loved so much. Very reminiscent of 1960's style lounges.

"Hmmm. Don't quite remember being this nostalgic." He commented, as he noticed the tacky coffee table, and the armchair.

Just then, he heard the front door open and he turned around quickly.

Fuck I hope that ain't me, he thought.

It wasn't.

To his surprise – and much delight – he saw Alison walk into the lounge.

"Oh, thank goodness you're home." She said, as she went up to him and kissed him on the cheek. "It's a frigging nightmare out there on the roads today," She went on as she started to pack groceries away, with him standing there, watching her, almost dumbfounded.

Am I dreaming?

"Apart from having to go meet Charles today and discuss the past due rent, the shopping was a nightmare," she went on, oblivious to the fact that the Alex that stood in the room was not the much younger version of himself, all those years before… Long before any of the events of Winmont had begun.

"I couldn't find a parking spot, then the checkout chick said there were problems with my card…" She paused long enough to let out a frustrated sigh, then went on, looking at him, "Anyway... how was your day?"

"Uh... Just fine I suppose." He replied, then went fully into the kitchen area where she was. He looked at Mattys' high-chair, then over at her.

She was just as young and beautiful as he remembered. If he could stay just in one period of time, he knew it would be here, right now. But he couldn't.

This was not real, it couldn't be.

But maybe it was. After all, he was thinking about this point in time just moments ago, when he was in the temple.

He hoped that this wasn't a dream. He knew this wasn't a memory, as this was the day before that fatal incident which sparked off the events that started him on the path he was to follow. He sighed, knowing what was to come. Her death, the death of his parents, the depression and alcoholism he would go through, his journey into the supernatural to find answers...

If he could prevent just one event from happening though, maybe, just maybe, things would be different.

Or would they?

He took a step closer and looked at her. She looked tired, stressed, but still had an ass that he could bang six ways from Sunday.

He went up to her and grabbed her hands, almost delicately.

"Here." He said softly.

"Alex? What are you doing?" She quizzed.

"Just let me." He said as he gently massaged her hands.

She closed her eyes, and let the sensation relax her. He always knew how to get one of her soft spots, and this was one of them.

"Babe, what are we going to do about..."

"Shhh," He interrupted. "Let's discuss it later."

"Matty..." She began.

"Our son is fine," He whispered, as he started to kiss her neck softly.

He wanted her, right now. He wanted, and needed to fuck her. Even just one last time.

"Alex, babe." She said softly, "Come on. Not now."

"But babe," He whispered, "I need."

"Alex. No." She said. But he didn't listen. He needed to feel close to her. Needed to feel how good he felt being inside her.

"Alex no!" She said sternly and pushed him away.

She ran her fingers through her hair and sighed heavily. "I love you Alex, but sometimes your timing is wrong... very wrong."

He looked away from her, almost shamefully. "Sorry." He said.

"Look, it... it doesn't matter. Maybe later, when I come home from Mother's tonight, okay." She said as she walked past him and went into the lounge to straighten things up.

He followed her into the lounge and questioned. "What? Today?"

"Alex," She said, "Why are you asking me like this is new news?" She started towards the bedroom, with him following her closely behind. "We already discussed this. I am going to my parents to get Matty so I can be back tonight to plan for the weekend."

"You can't!" He blurted out, paused, then went on, "I mean ... Not tonight... please."

She turned to him and asked, "Why not?"

He looked at her and wanted to tell her why she couldn't leave, but he couldn't bring himself to tell her the truth.

He shrugged and stood there, mouth agape, and didn't respond.

"Okay then." She said and went over to him. She kissed him softly on the lips, then went on, "I'll get Matty from mom's and come back tonight okay."

He nodded in agreement.

"Besides, there is something I need to tell you tonight when I get back" She smiled, as she grabbed a few clothes from Matty's room and started to the door.

Alex just watched her in silence. He knew what was coming, but there was nothing he could do about it.

"Okay baby. See you tonight." She said, as she kissed him and walked out the door. She did not know it, but today was the last day she would see the light of day.

"Or maybe not." He muttered, as she hurried to the door. "I can stop this."

Alex hurried out the door, with only one thing on his mind... To stop this event from ever happening.

He planned to go with her, that way he could prevent her death from ever happening, and he would have his idealistic life back.

But that wasn't to be.

⁓

HE LEFT THE apartment and instantly he was back in that room in the temple.

"What the fuck?" He muttered. "What is this? Some kind of mind-fuck?"

"No." He heard her voice from behind him.

"Nanomi." He remarked, as he turned to face her. "Was that a dream?"

She shook her head, "No."

"Then why?"

"You needed to see."

"I could have done without seeing that. Of all places and times, why show me the day she died?"

"So you could understand that there was nothing you could have done to prevent that path, which would bring you here."

He sighed and looked away.

She stepped over to him and touched his face gently. "You know why you are here."

He nodded and wiped the tears from his eyes and looked at her face. "Yeah. I guess."

She smiled, and in her eyes, he saw something that he had not seen in a long time... A very long time. Love.

He leaned in and kissed her, and it was reciprocated.

THEY MADE LOVE, and for the first time since Ali, he felt a real connection to another woman. With Kaz, he never felt anything that could be a tangible connection. It was more of mutual gratification, like primal beasts needing to get their rocks off by meaningless sex, or more to the point, the sex Alex had with Kaz was more of what he classified as *Porn Sex*, or enemies with benefits would be a more apt saying.

They lay together, on the floor, with her cuddled up to him. He felt that this was somehow... right.

Odd, that she was from the past, and he from a future – whatever future that was. But here, now, is where he was... with her.

LITTLE DID HE know that even though the intimacy they shared meant something to her, but it was also destined. Destined for him to be with her. Destined to make love to her. Destined to give her his seed right at the pivotal point when she was ovulating.

The journey of the last, she will bear a child from the One, and in her seed, the bloodline shall become as the stars.

—Azullrokr the Prophet

THEY GOT DRESSED, almost without saying a word, but the exchanged glances said it all, at least from her. She loved him, even if he didn't feel the same. It was true that he felt a connection to her, but he would hardly say that it was love. He fell for that one before, and he wasn't about to give in to *that* emotion easily.

"Apart from what we just shared, what's our next move." He asked.

"It's time." She said, "Come, we must hurry."

"Time? Time for what?" He almost protested.

"Come." She said as she grabbed him by the hand.

11

JAMIESONN STOOD BEFORE the fallen demigod and sneered. He was looking forward to this moment. In fact, he had been waiting for this for a long time. And now that he was here, he intended to make the most of it.

"Well?" Tanzac sneered, "Do you think …"

"Enough!" Jamiesonn yelled with authority.

Tanzac's legion took a step back and for a split second, fear gripped each one of them.

Tanzac saw that fear, and with one swift move, he kicked Jamiesonn across the throne room, sending him smashing through the hardened lava wall.

Jamiesonn got up, dusted himself off and vanished, instantly reappearing in the throne room.

"That's the one you get. Now it's my turn." He snarled. Immediately he raised his hand towards Tanzac and sent him hurdling head first into the throne, smashing it to pieces.

Jamiesonn lunged at him, and with a swift movement, punched Tanzac in his head with great force.

Tanzac growled in pain.

"Now you die." Jamiesonn snarled as he levitated off the ground and hovered above the once great beast.

Tanzac slowly started to rise, and glared intently at his old enemy.

He glared at this man and snarled evilly.

Before Tanzac could do anything, Jamiesonn clicked his fingers and immediately a power hit Tanzac and started to consume the great beast.

Jamiesonn levitated back to the ground and watched with insane delight as the beast of old was helpless against his power.

Rapidly, the dark power consumed him and with one final howl, it was over… Tanzac vanished into dust.

Tanzac was no more.

Jamiesonn stood for a moment and gloated in his handiwork, then hearing the faint noise of the legion behind him, he turned to them and gazed at them.

They feared him, and feared what he could do. Slowly, they started to back away. Their only intent right now was to flee.

"Wait! Don't go just yet! The fun is just about to start!" Jamiesonn quipped.

~

Jamiesonn's attack was swift and furious. With all the hatred unleashing from within him, he slaughtered, each one of Tanzac's powerful demons, his legions, and his fallen army of darkness. The attack was bloody, merciless, and yet, satisfying. And when it was over, all he could do was stand among the hell-fire and gloat in what he had done.

Jamiesonn could feel the souls of the dead in this place, and as much fun he would get by slaughtering these souls, including Usher and Drake, he knew he would have more fun by joining this realm to his.

Jamiesonn stood in the room where Tanzac once ruled the underworld and he gazed around, peering into every part of the dark realm.

Millions of souls were here in this place, and seeing their torment, he knew that this place offered nothing when it came to the real horrors and pleasure of the sadistic torment he had in store for each lost soul.

"It begins." He quipped, and with a clap of his hands, Tanzac's realm began to merge with his own, to become a part of his netherworld kingdom. The ground, walls and all in this place started to shake violently, while he stood there and laughed.

Here, in his world, the lost souls that were once Tanzac's would suffer a torment that each one of them could never imagine.

Jamiesonn smirked. He destroyed his nemesis and soon would be the Chosen.

"Laura!" He called out, "Come, there is mayhem to create!"

12

THROUGH THE SEERS Crystal in the room which she led him to, Alex witnessed everything that just happened, so did Nanomi. He turned to her and was in shock,

"I ... I can't believe it." He muttered.

"You see why you must continue." She said, looking at him. This being, Jamiesonn, needs to be stopped before he unleashes his own hell upon the earth."

Alex smugly laughed, "How can I do that, Nanomi? I don't even have half of the powers I once had."

"In time you will, and more so." She said. She paused and hesitated for a moment to continue on, then, "If this creature defeats you, not only will mortals suffer an eternity of darkness, but our bloodline will be no more."

Alex looked at her and frowned. He knew that there were others in this bloodline, and he also knew that Jamiesonn would go after them first if he got his victory.

"Even we," She continued, "will not be safe. We will suffer the same fate as those in your time. For he will want all of the people, including those before us. His darkness will span all of the creation, from the beginning to the last."

Alex paused, then said, "You are saying that he will be that powerful, to even enslave those of the past?"

She nodded, and he could see that she was afraid.

He turned his gaze back at the Seers Crystal. He knew that he couldn't let that happen. He took a deep breath and for now all he could do was watch as history began to unfold and one by one, the prophecies of Azullrokr began to manifest before his eyes.

He did not like what he saw. Jamiesonn was creating havoc in his own time, and what Alex saw, he didn't like one bit.

The murders, the slaughters, the mass killing of people just so he could get what he wanted... his own self gratifying glory.

As much as Alex wanted to intervene, he couldn't. It was not as though he didn't try. It was that the powers that be – his powers – wouldn't let him.

~

JAMIESONN'S REIGN OF terror started mildly enough. First, it was one victim here, another one there. Normally, victims brought to him by his illustrious Hell Vixens. As fun as it was for him to disembowel each new virgin, he found the taste of their agonising deaths almost unsatisfying.

The blood would pour freely to satisfy his vixens thirst, and lavish the taste they did. He took delight in both the death of each person and in the pleasure his vixens felt.

It was not enough though. He knew that it was time to make his presence known to the world.

With his Hell Vixens in tow, Jamiesonn started on one killing spree after another. First, starting with the residents of Winmont. In the dead of night, he slaughtered everyone in that town horrifically. Disembowelment, beheading, tearing off limbs... Nothing was out of bounds.

On that night, every man, woman and child had been slaugh-tered. Killing hundreds. The screams of their torment had filled the air, but there was no help for the victims. No police. No reporters. No witnesses. It was as though the massacre went unnoticed by the outside world.

~

JAMIESONN DECIDED TO up his ante. He knew that the only way to get his real exposure was to be seen, and with that he started his global mission of terror.

From the fall of the night to the rise of the sun, his rampage of horror hit one family after another. From Sydney to Moscow; From New York to Baghdad, he took delight in the massacre of both the innocent and corrupt alike. From those who were janitors to even heads of state. He slaughtered each person in the most horrific manner, and drank the blood of his victims. And just as easily as he would enter their residences, he would vanish.

13

It wasn't as though he wanted to slaughter as many people as he could for their warm blood. No, he left the dead for his vixens to finish off. He just wanted to be seen and make the world fear him.

There were always those tell-tale signs that he left behind in his wake. Namely, the CCTV footage that caught him on camera, in various parts of the world.

His actions were quickly noticed by local police officers, then when his face appeared in various footage around the world, that was when Interpol and other agencies of the world started to act. But, like the cunning bastard he was, he only allowed those in authority to get so close before he would turn and massacre them also.

Local police forces, FBI, MI6, SWAT. All fell to be victims of his horrendous crimes.

It was a bloodbath of the likes the world had not seen from any one man. And his attention seeking genocide did get the attention of the worldwide media, just as he intended from the beginning.

~

JAMIESONN STOOD ONCE again at that cliff and watched out over the ocean. As he stared, he knew that he was now the most hunted person in the world, and that made him smirk wickedly.

He peered into the events of what the media was saying about him. Much to his delight he could see that a lot of the media had dubbed him "Antichrist", while others called him the "Global Killer".

Laura walked up and stood near him, but said nothing.

"Do you see, daughter." He smugly said.

She turned her gaze to what he could see and she smiled.

"They have branded me a terrorist… Comparing me to the likes of the IS."

"I know, father." She said, "What shall be your will in this?"

He turned to her, smiled and remarked, "Time to turn myself in."

She frowned, and he touched her face softly,

"Don't be alarmed, dear daughter. You are powerful in the dark ways, but even I conceal things from you. In time, you will see why."

"As you wish." She said.

"Stay until I return." He said. With that, he looked past her then walked off, vanishing a moment later, with Laura looking back the way he left, then turned her focus back to the ocean. She had an idea of what was going on, but then again, Laura was becoming less content with being his mere puppet.

She was queen of his netherworld, but her hunger for more power was growing. She felt that hunger, and she did a damn good job at hiding that from her father.

She turned and walked away, and returned in an instant to the netherworld, where she sat down on his throne and looked out over the kingdom he had. This is what she desired, what she wanted.

~

JAMIESONN'S ARREST WAS uneventful to say the least. One minute, the FBI office in DC had several officers trying to co-ordinate a manhunt for the unnamed assailant, then the next Jamiesonn appeared in the room, much to everyone's surprise.

"I'm here. So, arrest me." He had said coyly, with his hands outstretched.

They had no clue how he had managed to walk past security downstairs, nor did they know how he managed to walk past every person in the building without being noticed. All they knew is that the world's most wanted criminal was there in front of them, now. That was an illusion that he made them see.

Jamiesonn was arrested, in a manner that even he knew was beneath him. No parade, no fan-fair, no mass media on the moment of his arrest. But that was the way he wanted to play his game.

Even when he was interrogated, he played his game and confessed to everything. He was shown photographs of his actions, footage, and all he said, and wanted to say was, "That's me. I did it. And you know what, I would gladly do it all again."

For the next 120 days, Jamiesonn was held in a maximum-security prison in an undisclosed location while the FBI built the case of the millennia against him. From the time of his arrest to the time he was transferred to the prison, the news of his incarceration had hit the media, and of course – just as he expected – that made global news. Not only would he be held on charges for mass murder in the US, but he was wanted by other authorities in Europe, UK, and Australia. Each country wanted him to stand trial for his crimes against humanity.

From the same day Jamiesonn was transferred to prison, he already had enemies on the inside. Not because the inmates knew who he *really* was, but because of the crimes he had committed, especially against children, some of the children were their own or related to them.

The inmates plotted to kill him off quickly. Little did they know that he knew what they were planning. He knew their thoughts, and the schemes, and when a few of them decided to act, a group of ten approached him. Their intent was to kill him, while the guards stood by and watched. The guards knew what was about to go down, after all, they supplied the knives for them to kill this inmate.

Jamiesonn stood and looked at each of them and smirked wickedly.

"You boys think you can come here to kill me." He mocked, as he glanced at them with a smile.

"Time to pay bitch, for killing my little girl!" One of them remarked, as he brandished the knife.

Jamiesonn said nothing. He knew what he was talking about, and he remembered murdering this inmates' teenage daughter. He looked at each of them with disgust and anger.

"Let's see if you squeal like a bitch…" He remarked coldly. Then he leaned in and went on, "Just like your little girl did when I raped her then drank her fresh warm blood."

The guards watched as the inmates yelled loudly and went to attack, but it was over all too quickly. Showing his true nature, Jamiesonn attacked each of the inmates and slaughtered them effortlessly. One, he tore his larynx out of his throat, another he snapped his neck, and another he ripped the heart out and devoured it within seconds.

Even the six guards didn't stand a chance up on the walkway. They went to open fire on Jamiesonn but it was too late. He leaped up to the walkway and killed the guards in the same horrific manner he loved to dish out to mortals, and when it was over, he stood there, blood dripping from his chin and glared at the rest of the inmates who stood back and could only look at the bodies that he had mutilated.

Jamiesonn breathed deeply, and looked at one of the cameras on the wall. He sneered and walked up to the nearby camera, grabbed it and stated,

"Know this. You will all fear me." He said before smashing the camera. He then turned and gazed down at the surviving inmates, and continued, "All you worthless mortals WILL fear me."

The inmates were afraid. He could feel their fear, and that fucking pleased him. Even those in the control room who witnessed what happened had begun to be afraid.

He wiped the blood from his face with the back of his hand and licked it off, savouring the taste. He jumped down to the ground, and glanced over at the other prisoners.

"From now on, you do my biding." He muttered, and immediately the eyes of each one of them turned black from the darkness. They were now his to control.

～ゥ

THE AUTHORITIES KNEW that this was too much for any one government to prosecute him, considering that good ol' Jamiesonn had already left tens of thousands dead in his wake. And now, he had murdered ten inmates and six guards.

Just as he expected, the prosecutor of the International Court got involved and he was transferred to the ICC's Detention Centre, in Hague.

Everything was going according to his own plan. Despite being treated less than an animal during the transfer from the US to Hague, he didn't give a fuck. This was how his fate was meant to be. As he awaited his new destination, he watched and searched the ages for Alex.

14

WEEKS PASSED, WITH no incidents out of him from inside the detention centre in Hague. Jamiesonn sat in his cell and awaited his day in court. He already knew the hysteria the media had created about him from the time he was first imprisoned, and that coverage only increased when it was leaked of what he did to the guards and inmates of that maximum-security prison – thanks to himself.

He knew that as the hysteria grew, and the coverage, so too would his fame and that made it all the more fun for him.

As much as anyone wanted to get him on TV – and many networks did try – he refused all of them... even the lawyer appointed to him recommended he go on TV to speak his voice, as an act to get people to sympathise with him. But Jamiesonn wouldn't have a bit of it.

With much persistence, his lawyer urged him to face the press. After all, he had committed mass murder, rape, torture, and numerous other acts of violence against humanity, and sooner or later, he needed to face the press at least once.

He was reluctant, but he nodded and gave his lawyer permission to have one person talk to him.

This is it.

~~

JAMIESONN SAT IN his cell that cold winter day, shackled and restrained to the cold chair.

As the cameraman set up his gear, he gazed at the reporter and smirked almost lustfully. He looked back out of the corner of his eye at the two elite SWAT guards who stood near the wall, both armed with AK47's, ready to act if anything went wrong.

He smirked wickedly then looked back at her, glaring intently at her and her soul.

"Connie." He said, "You're just as lovely and … soothing as my daughter."

Her stomach turned as his comment. As much as she wanted this interview with this … man, his stares and remarks turned her stomach.

Connie was a seasoned reporter, working for a tv series named *Most Violent Criminals* that aired in the greater Manchester area.

For all she accomplished in her career as a reporter, TV host, she was young, no older than 30 or 31. Long brown hair, blue eyes and considered attractive by many people, even herself. With her, business always came first, and she worked hard, and played harder. She was there to do a job, and one that she did quite well.

She sat opposite him, looked at her notes, and then looked back at him.

His interview was being televised live, and that was the one thing he wanted, and insisted on.

As Connie began her interview, he turned his focus between the camera and back at her.

"How many are watching this… charade." He commented, coldly.

"Ah, I don't know exactly." She said, "It is live, so could be thousands in Manchester."

"*Just* Manchester?" He blurted out, almost rising.

"Settle down!" One of the guards from behind him ordered.

He sneered and reclined back on the chair, disgusted.

"I...I don't know exactly." She stammered. "I ... I think this interview is over."

She started to get up, only to see Jamiesonn scream loudly and clench his fists.

"I will say when it over!" He screamed as loud as he could. At once the chains which bound him fell off him effortlessly like tissue paper, and he jolted up and turned to the guards. Before they could get a shot off, Jamiesonn picked up the chair, ripped it in half and stabbed both of them through the head.

He watched their lifeless bodies collapse to the floor, then turned his gaze to Connie and her cameraman, which were backed against the wall, both cowering and crying.

"Please don't. Don't kill me, I have... family." She whimpered.

"Good." He snarled as he stormed towards her, "Now I know who to massacre next!"

With one swift move, he grabbed both of them and dragged them in front of the camera and forced them on their knees.

With one look at the camera, he pointed his forefinger and in an instant, what was only airing live in Manchester started to stream live across the globe, on all TV channels, all social media. Everywhere there was a viewing audience, he was seen.

"Now people." He remarked sinisterly as he crouched down a little and looked into the camera, "Slime of this ... crude planet... You will recognise me as the worlds most wanted criminal. Today, you bitches, I am bringing you my new show, Reality TV Murders... I'm your host... you fuckers can call me... Jamiesonn."

With that, he grabbed Connie and her cameraman by the back of the head and made them look at the camera. They could do nothing but whimper.

"Today on my show, you get to see these two ... scum die." He remarked. "Connie here is an intrepid journalist. Wife to Teddy and mother of three ungrateful spoilt prissy brats." He paused and went on smartly, "I like them already." He looked over at Jorge, then back at the camera. "On my right is Jorge. A worthless piece of shit who lives with some idiot loser housemates. Jorge likes long walks on the beach, sunsets, and getting stoned. In his free time, he secretly frequents whores to get blown and spends his free time jacking off to online porn."

He paused again, just to gloat in what he was about to do. Jorge and Connie both pleaded for him to let them go, but that was not part of his agenda.

He tightened his grip on the back of their heads and with one forceful strike, he slammed both of their heads together with tremendous force. Those watching could hear the distinct sound of bones breaking and they watched in shock as he smashed their heads together repeatedly until their brains oozed out all over their lifeless body and onto the floor.

After he slaughtered Connie and Jorge, he looked at the camera, licked the blood and brains from his fingers.

"Tasty." He remarked. "Thanks for watching. On next weeks episode". He paused and looked up towards the door.

At that moment, the door burst open and yelling filled the room. The yelling from other SWAT ordering him to lay face down on the ground.

"Get down now!" They yelled.

Jamiesonn looked at them, there were ten of them in all, all armed with AK47s, with their weapons aimed right at his face.

He smirked. "Looks like we have more guests for this episode."

He stood quickly and lunged at the guards, knocking the camera down in the process.

To the audience, they could not see anything. The only thing the audience heard was the mass of gun-fire and terrifying screams, then moments later, silence. Absolute fucking silence.

A few more moments later, footsteps were heard, then seen in front of the camera. At once the camera started to rise from the ground, moving slowly up the body until only his face was seen in the camera, and to those who were watching.

He smiled, evilly at the viewers. "Thanks for tuning in." He remarked and punched the camera hard, making it smash into pieces.

The live feed stopped, and only static was seen for some moments before normal broadcasting continued.

~ 9

ALEX TURNED TO Nanomi and shook his head in disgust.

"He needs to be stopped."

"I know." She said, as she gently touched his arm, "Your time will come."

Alex looked at her and suddenly started to feel strange... light-headed.

"Nanomi...." He said, "Wh-what is ..."

Alex looked at his hands to see them start to disappear before his eyes.

First, his hands, arms, then the rest of him slowly disappeared, and not by his own power.

"Nanomi?" He called, but even his voice faded out. She only looked at him, with concern in her eyes. She knew what was happening. Prophecy was starting to come to an end.

"I love you, Alex." She whispered, as he vanished. She hung her head, sad, that he was gone from her side. But she knew she carried a part of him in her womb. She placed a hand on her stomach and rubbed it gently.

"Your line will continue." She said softly, with a smile.

~ 9

JAMIESONN SAT IN his cell and waited for the charade that was next. He knew that his face was now the only thing on TV, but that still was not enough. He needed to make these people – the whole world – see exactly who he was and what he was capable of.

He sat on the floor, legs crossed, and whistled a little random tune as he waited.

He could have left that place anytime he wanted to and returned to his own world, but that would be far too easy. Besides, what fun would that be? He loved playing with these mortals. He enjoyed mind-fucking them maybe a little too much.

15

Laura saw what her father did, and she sneered with disapproval. "Why should daddy have all the fun." She remarked, as she walked off to where Usher was experiencing a hell like nothing before. She was annoyed, pissed off even. She felt that he was stealing all the lime-light while she stayed at *home* like a common *lady-in-waiting*.

Yes, she was pissed. And the angrier she got, the more her own power grew.

In an instant, she appeared in the hell Usher was experiencing and glanced around. The room was similar to what Usher had been in ever since he was transported to Tanzac's world, but ever so different.

The walls dripped molten lava, and the floor was that of glass, exposing a burning pit below. The floor was almost fragile, and to Usher, any sudden movement from him would mean his eternal death.

Usher saw her, but he had no clue who she was. All he knew at that moment was that she looked like a wanna be goth, with dark hair, dark mascara and black dress. Usher feared for his life. He didn't want to die, if in fact he was truly dead.

"Please." He begged her, "Don't come in here."

She huffed and walked towards him.

"Please!" He called out, "The floor… it's…"

She stopped and retorted, "What? The floor is what, Usher?"

He looked at her, strangely and wondered how she knew his name.

She walked closer to him. The floor was fragile, but to her it was anything but.

"The floor is what?" She almost seemed to demand.

He couldn't answer. He could only stand on that chair and cringe.

She stopped a few feet away from him and looked at him.

"Pffft. To think," She started, "you, the once great man of vision, now trapped and cowering like the worthless worm you are."

He shook his head. The heat in the room was enough of a mind-fuck as it was, without her taunts to add to it.

"You're not real." He began to mutter over and over.

She looked at him with raised eyebrow and said, "Oh… really." She looked at the floor beneath them both then back at him and smiled wickedly.

Usher knew that look. He had seen that look before, but not from her.

"Jamiesonn…" The words escaped his mouth.

"Wrong, but close enough." She retorted. With that she raised one hand and made a ball with her fist.

Usher knew what she was going to do. "Please, not like this." He pleaded, "I can't go out like this."

She never replied. She just smiled that wicked look of hers and slammed her fist on the ground as hard as she could. The ground began to tremble beneath him and started to crack.

"NO!" He screamed, crying, "Not like this!"

It was too late. She slowly stood upright and watched with insane pleasure as the floor underneath him cracked open and started to fall apart.

Laura glared at him and remarked coldly, "Don't forget to tell Apportioner I said '*hi*'"

Usher screamed as the floor beneath him gave way and she watched with that insane delight as he fell helplessly into the burning pit below. His screams echoed and filled her ears with euphoria. Then, the silence. He was dead…

She smiled, and turned and walked off.

She hated sitting around doing nothing. Part of her felt like a fucking patsy. Being the girl she was, she wasn't going to sit around and do jackshit.

At once she vanished from the netherworld and appeared in the world of the mortals.

16

LAURA STOOD ON the roof of the largest building in the city and breathed in the scent of the population. She smelled their fear in the darkness of the night, and that filled her with excitement.

She gazed ahead and could see, far in the distance – many thousands of miles away – her father being led into the court-room. The plans of her father were going according to what he planned, but now was her time.

She wanted this... she damn well deserved it!

~

WITH A WAVE of her hand, three Hell Vixens appeared behind her, bloodthirsty and awaiting her bidding.

"Go." She said, motioning with her hand, "Feast."

At once the three vixens soared down into the streets to start their feasting on any mortals they wanted.

Screams started to fill the night air, and the sounds of her vixens screeching, as they attacked each new victim.

"Father dear," She commented with a smirk, "You're not the only one who can create fear in mortals."

~

As JAMIESONN STOOD in the court room, bound in shackles, his attention went to that of Laura.

Through the vast miles, he heard her, and he smugly smiled.

Go. He thought to her, *Go and slaughter them.*

Jamiesonn turned his attention back to the judge. He knew this judge's secrets, he knew his thoughts, his deepest desires, his ... secret sins.

He glanced around the room slowly, noticing everyone there. The three guards that stood near the wall, the two prosecutors, and even the court reporter. In an instant, he knew all their darkest secrets, all their hidden sins. But the one man who mattered in that room – apart from himself – was that judge. That was the one Jamiesonn needed most.

Judge Reginald Akari was a middle aged, well respected man in the international community, and some would consider him a leader. But, even as clean as his life appeared to be, with a wife of thirty years, six grown children and a pet Labrador – who was advanced in years – he had his own dark secrets that not even his closest friends or family knew about.

"How do you plead?" He asked.

Jamiesonn knew those dark secrets of his, and intended to use them against him.

"How do you plead?" He was sternly asked again.

"I confess. I am guilty as sin." Jamiesonn said smartly. He leaned forward slightly on the desk and paused long enough to make his fact crystal clear, then went on with power in his tone, "But, you ... Reggie... are going to acquit me of all charges." He paused again, just long enough to reveal to this esteemed judge's mind the dark secrets of his past. The bribes he took, the teenage boys he molested in his younger years, the secret affairs behind his wife's back… even the abuse of his own daughter which started when she was ten years old.

He turned his gaze over to the prosecutors and immediately, those secrets that they had hidden for many years were revealed to their mind, instantly causing them fear this *man of perdition.*

He looked back at the judge and glared at him. "Yes…" Jamiesonn spoke to his mind, "I know your sins… And so will the multitude."

"As for you two." He said, looking back at the two prosecutors, "You two shall drop all charges."

With that, he took his seat and bellowed proudly, "Do what you will!"

For a moment, the two prosecutors and the judge were dazed, then when they came around, the judge glanced over at the prosecutors, then the defendant.

"Do you have anything to add?" He asked the lead prosecutor.

"Nothing, your honor." He stammered.

"Then I have no choice but to proclaim you not guilty." The judge said, then he hit the gavel on the block, "Dismissed." He stated.

Jamiesonn smirked wickedly. *At last. Now they will see.* He thought.

With that he stood up, and glanced down at the shackles that bound him. At once they fell off, and he was free… not that he didn't know that already.

Jamiesonn walked out of the court room, in a sense of impending victory. He sensed what was coming.

With not a care in the world, he walked out of the building and gazed around at the crowd of the hundreds of people that stood there. Reporters and camera crew from various global media were there, close to the front of the crowd. They had been awaiting the verdict on this mass murderer.

When they saw him leave the building and stand there before them, free, a momentary silence broke over the crowd, as each person was shocked that he was allowed to be free.

He laughed to himself and continued down the stairs. Through the screaming protesters, he could hear the reporters throwing all kinds of questions at him. He ignored everyone's taunts, their comments, their ridicule. He didn't give a damn about what any of them thought.

Suddenly, as he approached the bottom of those stairs it happened. A single loud gunshot rang out, and a moment later, he fell lifelessly to the ground. People screamed and started to run off, but some stopped as they took a moment to glance at the body which lay in a thick pool of blood at the bottom of the stairs.

An eerie silence broke out over the crowd.

Was he dead? After all this, was Jamiesonn dead?

~

ONLY A FEW moments past, as his body lay on the steps, with blood oozing from his head. It was obvious that whoever the gunman was, their aim was accurate and true.

~

HE OPENED HIS eyes and began to stir, and taking a very brief moment, he got to his feet slowly and stood before the crowd.

Fear gripped each person there as they watched in awe as the bullet wound, which made a clean hole right through his head, sealed up before their – and everyone else who were watching around the world – eyes.

He laughed mockingly at them, raised one hand and clicked his fingers. In an instant, he was gone.

Those who witnessed the event, and everyone else who watched in on TV began to wonder to themselves; *Who is like this man and who could possibly make war on him?* While others who held religious beliefs thought; *Is he the Antichrist spoken of?*

In the days of his persecution he shall be struck down. Like one to bear a mortal wound to its head. He shall arise and all who see shall know the Son of Perdition has come.

—Azullrokr the Prophet 21:8.
Book of Mezunabite. 5,308BC

He was known to the world, and people feared him greatly. Which is what he wanted from the very beginning, even back many centuries ago when this path of his began.

17

ON THE OTHER side of the world, a violent storm raged in the heavens. Torrential rain poured down hard from the night sky, the loud sounds of thunder filled the night, and lightning charged across the clouds.

The local weather forecasters had no clue what was happening, as according to the forecast under an hour before it was meant to be a clear night on this night of the lunar eclipse.

Harder and harder the rain fell all over the city and outskirts, causing flash flooding, and in some places, landslides.

Commuters hurried to get to their destinations as fast as they could to escape the rain, but it seemed futile. With each passing moment, the rain came in harder and stronger, as did the wind from the East.

> When the moon is in the full and filled of blood, the waters from above shall burst forth to drench the new lands, and with it the winds of the East shall tear down their kingdoms, until that of the past has come again to his own to stand one time last against the beast of the night

THE STRENGTH OF the wind and rain only increased, as lightning started to strike various parts of the city. Some lightning struck trees, another strike demolished a house, another violent strike demolished a ten-story building, and another struck a lone gravesite in a forgotten cemetery. The tombstone exploded violently, in an array of dirt, dust and cement. As the dust started to settle, a lone figure stood there, standing amongst the rubble with his head faced down.

He stepped forward from the debris and turned his gaze towards the sky. At once, as though by his unheard order, the winds, the rain, the storm ceased, revealing the blood red moon in the sky and the beauty of the night.

He knew the destruction that both Jamiesonn and Laura had caused in both of their violent rampages, and all he could feel was sorry for these mortals.

"Time to set things right." He remarked, as his eyes glowed as bright as blue sapphires.

"Alex…" He heard his name being called from across the realms. He glanced back, knowing it was Nanomi. He could see her standing in that room, with one hand on the Crystal. She had tears in her eyes. He smiled at her, and whispered, "Remember me."

I will, her voice echoed in his mind.

He turned, and looked straight ahead of him. He sensed danger. That danger was close, and that threat was Jamiesonn.

"Time to end this now, Jamiesonn." He said, and walked off. He knew where the dark prince was hiding, and it wasn't in his own realm.

IT WAS NO surprise that up until now, Alex had been a pawn in the game of the Elders. Even the powers he had previously were limited at best. Fuck, even after he walked away, from everything, he could have been beaten the shit out of by any drunken bitch in a bar. Even in his own recent timeline, he could have been killed easily by his alter ego, but that is not how the Elders played this game against the Darkness.

In this time, this era, is when those abilities of his had been restored by the Elders to face the Darkness, just one last time.

The moment that he manifested on the place of his own grave, was the moment that he became just as powerful as the Elders once were, before they were transcended into the Light Beings that Alex, and many others, knew.

Now, whatever happened was his own prophecy. This was his prophecy, and the destiny he was meant to fulfil by the Elders.

But the Darkness, the Son of Perdition, the Serpent of Old… Had his own prophecy.

18

No sooner had Alex vanished, when he reappeared in the clearing outside Winmont.

He glanced around the destroyed ruins and took it all in. The once great pillars Tanzac had put up were long gone, and the ground was now no more than mere hardened red dirt... lifeless, barren, void of any kind of life.

"I expected you to be hiding out somewhere with more... style." Alex remarked, as he couldn't help but see the funnier side of this place. For a moment, it almost reminded him of a scene he saw in a movie once or twice, or maybe two hundred times.

"I thought you'd like it." He heard Jamiesonn say from nearby.

Alex turned his gaze to the tree line ahead and watched as Jamiesonn walked out from behind one of the trees and approached him.

"I see you finally have come into your own." Jamiesonn remarked, sensing the great power that Alex now had.

"Still the narcissistic prick, no less." Alex replied, "But where, oh where is that ... slut daughter of yours." He paused to peer into the darkness of the forest beyond the clearing, then turned his gaze back to Jamiesonn. He gazed over at him then gazed around, his eyes looking back and forth. He knew she was there, lurking in the background.

"I know she's here… Come out, come out, wherever you are." He almost sang, leaning back smartly, then started to circle his old nemesis.

Jamiesonn glared intently at him. He knew the power this man now possessed, and one thing was for certain, no one, not even the *Great Alex*, would stand in his way.

"Come now…Old friend." Jamiesonn said, "You know that you are out-matched. Remember kid, I saved your fucking ass from a mere fucking doppelgänger." He finished, mocking him.

Alex looked at him with a glint in his piercing eyes. "Maybe." He commented, then with hands outstretched, said "But, here I stand. Now. Before you, and very much alive as you are."

Jamiesonn sneered at him. "So be it. Chosen One." He remarked spitefully, and lunged at him with incredible speed.

Alex instinctively raised his hand, and immediately time seemed to slow down. Alex slowly lowered his hand and looked oddly at his adversary, as he almost floated in mid-air.

These powers, these new powers, he found mind boggling. Not only could he journey to whatever time period he wanted, but it also seemed that he could stop time momentarily if he wanted. These new powers he liked, a little too much.

He walked out of the way of the oncoming attack and watched as Jamiesonn landed on his front, in almost slow motion.

In a second, the effect wore off, and Jamiesonn rolled on the ground, and stood up just as fast.

"Impressive kid." He remarked, as he regained that composure of his.

Alex smirked at him with eyebrow raised.

They started to circle one another, slowly, like they were both sizing up one another. Little did they know that Laura was there, waiting, to strike on her father's command.

"You have come a long way, kid." Jamiesonn stated, "But your journey has come to an end."

"Oh, I don't think so." Alex replied. With a strike of his own, he raised his hand and sent Jamiesonn flying across the clearing a good ten to fifteen feet away. Jamiesonn landed heavily on the ground, shaken, but far from beaten.

Fuck he's good. He thought, as he stood up quickly. He knew that he needed to up his game if he was to defeat this Chosen One, and that he did.

With a thought, a sole thought, he summoned his Vixens.

Almost instantly four elite assassin Vixens appeared in the clearing, surrounding Alex. One in each direction.

Alex looked around quickly at them. Knowing the power each one of them possessed, he could only brace himself for what was to come. He remembered these bitches, from another time, another place. But this… this was different to say the least. These hot vamps were nothing like the bitches of the mist he once encountered. These vixens possessed strength and power that Tanzac's brood never did.

They began to circle him, in unison… almost in formation, all the while hissing and snarling at him as Jamiesonn came into view and watched his prize *ladies* slowly circled in for the kill.

Alex looked in each direction quickly. He could see that these voluptuous vixens from hell were slowly closing in on him as they circled him.

Was he afraid? No. Not in the least. Did he want to fuck each one of them? That thought had crossed his mind once, twice, or more than a few times already.

Alex crouched forward just a little and watched them circle him.

"Skanks." He muttered, then jumped well clear of them effortlessly, landing on his feet away from the clearing, and started to run off.

Jamiesonn nodded at them, and at once they pursued Alex into the darkness of the night.

~ ⁹

ALEX STOPPED RUNNING and turned to face the oncoming Vixens. This was what he needed, to be a good distance away from Jamiesonn before he could retaliate, on his own terms.

He stood and waited for those vixens to attack, and this time, in the darkness of night, he would be able to fight on his own terms.

He stood upright, peered toward the clearing, closed his eyes and vanished, but he was far from gone from this time.

The Vixens swiftly arrived to where he was last seen, but nothing. They couldn't see him anywhere in the darkness of the forest.

Alex opened his eyes, and he could see them as plain as day.

"I see you." His voice echoed from all around them.

They snarled and glared around, and again, they couldn't find him. Even with their unholy powers could they see him.

"I'm over here." His voice whispered from one direction. "Over here." He whispered from another direction. "No. Over here skanks." His voice whispered yet again from another direction.

They screeched angrily at his taunts.

He saw their insanity, their anguish of not being able to find him, and in a perverse way, that pleased him.

"No, here." He said from the midst of them. Quickly they turned around, and for a second they saw him standing right behind them, and the next second he was gone again.

"Ahhhh!" One of them screeched, "Find him!"

Alex immediately appeared in the bushland nearby, and he crouched down and watched silently as the vixens continued to search valiantly for him. The last thing they wanted to do was fail their Master, and they knew that any form of failure – especially in a matter like this – meant extreme torture for these women.

ALEX STAYED WHERE he was, crouched in the thicket of the bushland, and watched these Vixens scour the area for him. Neither with their eyes, nor their abilities, could they find him.

He smiled, almost smugly, as they searched frantically for him.

He turned his gaze elsewhere, and could see Jamiesonn, in the distance, pacing up and down, almost like an impatient tiger ready for his meal.

"Keep dreaming dickhead." He muttered, as he looked back to the vixens. But still, even with his power, he could not sense Laura, but he knew that she was there. Just hidden from his senses.

He huffed. He didn't like not being able to sense her presence, when he knew that she was there, somewhere, lurking in the darkness.

He glanced around again, and seeing them coming closer to his direction, he threw another distraction, this time, a sound from a distance behind them.

Immediately they turned and scurried off towards that sound, thinking that it was Alex.

"Idiots." He muttered, as he slowly stood up and watched them hurry away from him.

"Not." He heard a voice say right behind him, and a sharp object being pierced into his lower back, "As much idiots as you thought, huh…"

He slowly raised his hands above his head and he sighed heavily.

"Okay Laura", He remarked. "Let's go confront your dear ole daddy shall we."

Laura shoved him forward and Alex obeyed. After all, he knew fucking damn well what she was holding in her hand. That legendary *Dagger of Legion*. The same damn golden-handled dagger that Jamiesonn had so many years ago, when this whole shit started. That dagger held the power to kill him, Jamiesonn or Elders alike.

"Move" She demanded.

Alex staggered forward, with hands above his head, like a prisoner of war, back to that clearing.

C.A.Milson

"Well... Alex." Jamiesonn said smugly, "Glad to see you have returned for the next round."

Alex slowly lowered his hands and watched them both carefully.

"Laura." Jamiesonn almost ordered his daughter.

She sighed, muttered something under her breath and went to stand beside her father, with the dagger still in her hands.

"And now... It comes to the end." Jamiesonn stated. With a click of his finger, all of them, including his vixens, were instantly transported to his own realm, to his own throne room.

Alex glanced around slowly, and he saw how this place had changed dramatically.

"I see you have upgraded this joint." He remarked, then said smartly "I take it this is the Jamiesonn Windows ME edition?"

Jamiesonn sneered and outstretching his hand, he threw Alex with great force against one of the walls.

Alex, stunned from the blow, slowly rose to his feet and turned to face his enemy.

"Yeah... Okay..." he stammered, "I'll give you that one."

The four Vixens grabbed him harshly and threw him to the centre of the throne room.

Jamiesonn glared at him. This kid certainly had power, that he could sense. But, he sensed something else... something ... darker... but yet... confusing.

Jamiesonn turned back to Laura, and seeing the look in her eyes, he turned to Alex and remarked, "Nice try kiddo. But turning my own blood against me shall never work."

With that, he again stretched out his hand and black lightning emanated from his fingers, instantly engulfing Alex in a shroud of impenetrable darkness. He fell to the floor, writhing in pain.

"Struggle as you will... Chosen." Jamiesonn remarked coldly, "But from this there is no escape."

Try as he might – and he did really struggle – Alex could not break free from this dark power that had engulfed him. He fought, and even tried to teleport out of there, but the darkness was too overpowering.

Gradually, slowly, he was beginning to die. He knew he was. He closed his eyes and focused harder, but try as he might, he was fighting a losing battle.

Nanomi! Azullrokr! He screamed in his mind, but to no avail. No one, nothing could hear his screams, his pleas of agony, as this powerful force started to worm its way into his body, his heart, his very soul.

He looked at Jamiesonn, his captor, and could only fear for the safety for the rest of humanity. This was what it was all about... Saving humankind from this dreaded beast.

With a look, a gaze, he focused his attention to Laura. He was dying, and there was nothing that he could do about it.

He focused what power he had left, and glared right at her.

Laura, His thoughts finally able to penetrate her mind, *See the truth.*

~

IN A TWINKLING of an eye, in a split second in time, Laura saw – for the first time – the truth... In that split moment ...

she saw everything that happened years ago .... For the first time, the truth of what Jamiesonn did to Tony – her beloved – was revealed.

Tony ... She muttered under her breath. She looked at Jamiesonn – her father – then looked at the dagger in her hands. Tears swelled in her eyes as she glanced up at Alex.

Alex stretched out his hand to her, but it was too late for him. His race was over in this apocalypse. With a final breath, a final deep breath, he exhaled and succumbed to the dark force that sucked the fucking life out of him.

Alex was... dead. No force, neither of the present, past or future would be able to save him.

Prophecy was... Fulfilled.

~

JAMIESONN YELLED WITH excitement and did a little celebration jig, knowing that he had finally killed Alex – the Chosen One of the Elders – not even noticing that Laura was standing nearby with that fucking dagger in her hand.

Again, she glanced at Alex, then at her father, then back at Alex.

What have I… She began to think. But Jamiesonn didn't notice. He didn't notice in the least. He was too much in the moment from having finally triumphed over the Chosen One. Even his precious vixens were too busy in the moment to realise what was going on around them.

Rage filled her veins, her thoughts, her very actions. She glared at her father with extreme hatred, and as he turned to her, laughing in triumph, she struck at him with extreme vengeance. "You son of a bitch!" She screamed with fury as she stabbed him as hard as she could through his cold dark heart, and again stabbed him, yelling. "This is for what you did to Tony!"

Jamiesonn screamed, in pain… real pain… as he collapsed on his back to the floor, as a cold black mist emanated from his body and vanished above him.

He gasped for breath, as black blood started to spurt from his mouth.

What the hell fuck, he could only think, as he lay there on the floor, dying. *Traitor…*

"L-Laura…" He spurted, reaching up for her. She glared at him, wickedly, and felt nothing for him. No sorrow, no remorse. Nothing.

"Time to end father." She commented, as she lunged one final time and stabbed him with that dagger through his head fiercely.

Jamiesonn crippled, spasmed, and with a final gasp of his breath he whispered, "Anarchy will prevail!" With that he died.

Laura slowly stood up, with dagger in hand and glanced around. She was tearful, afraid, upset, angry. She looked at the vixens with tears in her eyes. They backed away from her ever so slowly. They sensed the great deal of anger inside her, but also a sense of humanity she still remained within her. They wanted to retaliate, but they couldn't. She was their Queen, their ruler, their... Master.

Laura walked over to the balcony and gazed across the land that was formerly Jamiesonn's kingdom, which was now hers. She could see the tortured souls of the dead. She could also see humanity in the real world and the aftermath of what her father had left behind.

"What is your bidding, Master?" One of the Vixens hissed.

Laura turned to them, glanced at the dead bodies of Alex and Jamiesonn, then slowly turned back to the hellfires she saw before her. "Dispose of them in the pits." She merely coldly said, clutching that sacred dagger tightly.

"And then...?" Another asked.

Laura managed a wry smile, and commented, "You'll see... You'll see..."

She stood there, staring out over this kingdom of hers. She smirked, knowing damn well she was more powerful than what her father ever was, and as long as she held that sacred *Dagger Of Legion*, she would always be ... unstoppable. But ... thanks to Alex, there was that one shred of humanity that would always remain with her forever, that one thought lingering, haunting, the back of her mind... *Tony*.

The fate of the world was... unknown....

THE END

The Dagger Of Legion

One of a kind dagger.
This piece was loaned to me as a source of inspiration.

About the Author

C.A. MILSON BEGINNINGS started in 1989, when he lived in a small town in South Victoria, called Winchelsea ("Winch"), where for a time, he lived on a piggery farm.

The very first story he wrote was titled "Shack Of Evil", a horror short story of 9 pages, based on a "would be" paranormal investigator, who goes out to research a haunted shack. Those characters would later become the focus in the award winning series, "*Rise Of The Darkness*", "*Bloodline Of Darkness*", "*She's Not So Ordinary*", and the final book in the series, "*Prophecy's End*".

Presently, C.A. Milson spends his time between Australia, the Philippines and soon his journey will take him to the UK.

www.ingramcontent.com/pod-product-compliance
Lightning Source LLC
Chambersburg PA
CBHW030654110726
47901CB00002B/710